RESTORE YOUR DREAMLAND

restore your *Dreamland*

17 stories on the mysteries, wonders
and science of sleep

DR. YASSER NEGM

Editor: Sarah Chalmers
Interior designer: Eldar Huseynov
Cartoon artist: Tommy Sutanto
Cover designer: Ahmed Negm

Restore Your Dreamland
17 stories on the mysteries, wonders and science of sleep

ISBN   979-8-57880-927-9
ASIN   B08Q3QH6WV

DEDICATION

By her sweet beauty, I shut my eyes every night
By her adorable soul, I open my heart every morning
She has been the core of my day dreams for so long
She is often a joyful entry to my sweet night dreams
She is the Pacific island for my nightmares,
awake and asleep alike
For many years, she has been the pleasant share of my bed,
Which I as well wish for the rest of my days.
To my delicate half, Ghada.

THIS BOOK

This book is fiction and non-fiction, mysteries and Science, myths and facts.

It asks questions like, why did Michael Jackson's eyes stop dancing 60 days before his demise?

It asks you to imagine yourself as Crescendo, the caveman living in a 21st-century luxurious hotel or as part of a jury sentencing a criminal whose lawyer has been drowsy all throughout the trial.

In a journey through 17 stories, some fiction while others are real, this book explores the mysteries, wonders and science of sleep.

We'll go back to the 17th century to live the story of Titus and Arabella and we'll roam the streets of Victorian London with Charles Dickens.

We'll find out some amazing answers to some intriguing questions. Such as: What is the dilemma with generation X ladies? How many youths and children die due to poverty of time?

Is Thomas Edison a superman or a hypocritic sleeper? Is it a good idea to start the school day late?

You'll be intrigued to read the confessions of night shift doctors, the tale of a 2020 sleeping beauty, and the stories of the slumber murderer and the slumber artist.

How have big dreams changed our world? Can dreams empower your productivity and creativity?

Finally, in the last story, you'll take a cruise down the river Glymph.

As you may have already realized, all 17 stories center on one theme: sleep.

As the first in the "RESTORE" series, the end of the book outlines a 10-dimension plan to invest in the one third of your lifetime the sleep comprises to boost the other two thirds, for excellent results.

ABOUT THE AUTHOR

Dr Yasser Negm, an Egyptian-British writer, is a practicing medical consultant in the fields of pediatrics and pediatric gastroenterology. He has worked in Egypt, the United Kingdom, and the United Arab Emirates for more than 25 years. He is a fellow of the Royal College of Paediatrics and Child Health (RCPCH) in London and member of the European Society of Pediatric Gastroenterology, Hepatology, and Nutrition (ESPGHAN).

His comprehensive book on the coronavirus pandemic, *Covidians & Covidology,* gained 5-star ratings on Amazon and Goodreads and is available in both electronic and paperback versions.

Dr Negm has also penned various writings about his visions and views on public affairs. He has no affiliation to any organizations or institutes of any type except for medical professional societies.

You can check out Dr Yasser Negm's curriculum vitae on LinkedIn:

https://www.linkedin.com/in/yasser-negm-967135145/

He has a website (*yassernegm.com*) for his writings in Arabic, which contains more than 500 articles, stories, reports, audio, and videos.

Dr Negm's Facebook page (*https://www.facebook.com/DrYasser.Negm/*) has more than 129,000 followers.

As a Healthcare professional, Dr Negm has long term interest in sleep; the body and brain function during the night and its effect on creativity and productivity. In addition to his concerns about the adverse consequences of sleep disruption, such interest has motivated Dr Negm to write this book. Being fond of story-telling, simplifying scientific facts to the public, repudiation of myths, and cresting with a practical concise plan for restoration, the author has compiled his own cocktail recipe in this book.

TABLE OF CONTENTS

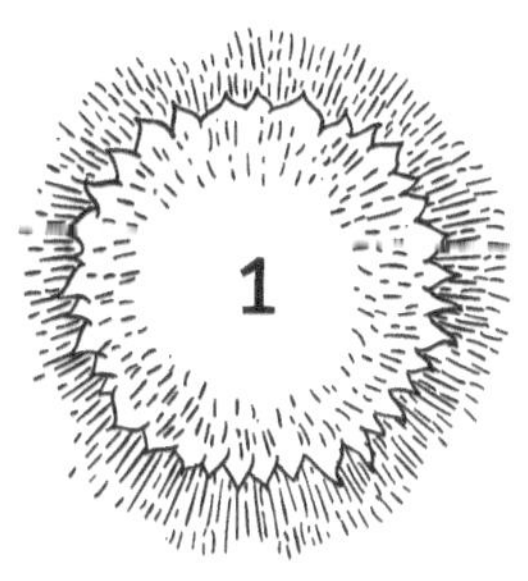

CRESCENDO

Out of breath, I stop. I can't even call on him to wait for me. I just wave and bend forward, panting. My God! He is too fit to keep up with. Crescendo disappeared between the colossal trees of the woods. What should I do now?

The most plausible option is to sit and wait.

I sit leaning against the nearest tree.

Have I lost him?

Whatever happens, I'll never return. But I am sure, he'll come back to find me. Crescendo always brings these pleasant little surprises.

***

Two months back, I was introduced to him for the first time, on that week when he was the most famous person on the planet, with media coverage of his appearance everywhere:

"A giant caveman found hiding in Jaco island!"

This was the first lie. He was not hiding. He was just peacefully living lonely there, until his nest was invaded by oil seekers. For how long had he lived there? Nobody knew, but probably for most of his life. He did not understand or speak any identified language, instead having his own jargon; he was 2.3 meters tall and barely wearing any clothes; and he did not have any tools of modern life. So, the "giant caveman" part was more or less spot on.

I was chosen to mentor him.

Why me? Well, they said:

"We acknowledge your top communication qualifications and vast experience as a special needs head teacher."

And this was the second lie; I was selected as an exile to relieve the headache I had been causing for the department due to my protest activity.

The timing was right for me. An "escape"—as described by my psychologist—is what I need to help my hypersomnia[1], which I knew was possibly an early symptom of depression.

Still...What exactly were they expecting me to teach him?

"Everything, Adam, everything," they said when I enquired about this. "English, manners, the ABC of modern life..."

"But why do we have to remain on this campus?" I asked.

They answered that the campus would be Crescendo's temporary residence for the sake of protection and research. For me, SEZRAS (The Secure Zone for Research and Science) was just a prison.

So, I'd ended up escaping into a prison. Well.

"Let's see how it goes," my pragmatic mind consoled me.

---

1   Hypersomnia is a disorder of excessive time spent sleeping, excessive sleepiness or a state of lack of alertness during the waking episodes of the day. It is not to be confused with fatigue, which is a normal physiological state.

The very first encounter occurred in his room, a seven-star hotel room luxury, well adapted to his hugeness. They thought this was the way to entice the guy into modern life; I was not sure that this was the right approach.

My room was next to his and exactly the same. Would that help my hypersomnia?

"Mmmmmm, probably not," I thought.

When I first saw him in the flesh, he was standing there, looking out the window at the open green landscape, probably thinking that was where he belonged. My God, he was reaaaally tall, and muscular by virtue of the nature-immersed style in which he had been living. He had a blend of a natural olive complexion and a tan with few scars here and there. His long semi-curly hair lacked care. I made some clatter to grab his attention.

"Hello. I am Adam, your new friend". I was talking to myself, as he does not understand English.

The man turned around, started to make very low noises in his jargon language, and then gradually but quickly raising the speed and the volume of these noises until they become really scary; a crescendo. Hence, this was the name I chose for him.

I was startled for a moment. He looked a decade younger than me; late thirties maybe. His childish features that appeared from between and beneath his massive facial hair seemed to be relaxed and sociable. So, I responded with a smile and then used all my experience dealing with primitive linguistics to communicate. It took a while, with a mixture of sign dialect, natural voices and instinctive body language. But slowly, it started to work.

Over the next few days, Crescendo and myself got along really well. He used to call me "Ada" and I did not bother to correct him. Our relations developed into a friendship smoothly and deeply. To my surprise—and against my outlooks—my hypersomnia improved significantly. I would wake up early, excited for new interactions and activities with Crescendo. I wouldn't go back to my bed unless I was really tired. Yet, Crescendo's interactions with the environment and people (other than me and Natalie, the cleaner servicing his room) were not that great.

For the most part, Crescendo did not like to stay in the luxurious room. He was allowed to go out with me, but with guards following us. He did not like them and was often aggressive towards them, chasing them around with his "crescendo" sounds. Whenever there were other residents of the campus outside, Crescendo would resist going out. He also disliked the seven-star hotel bed with the comfy mattress and preferred to sleep on the carpet (still much cozier if compared to the earth of the cave or the jungle). I ordered all tech gadgets out of the room including the TV, but even a basic contemporary requirement like a toilet seat, shower or sink were a struggle for him. No staff were allowed in the room except for Natalie. He trusted no one but me.

The situation was deteriorating. So, I asked for a meeting with Anthony, the campus manager.

"He is not coping. We need to do something," I told Anthony as soon as I sat down in his office.

"Well. To be honest, Mr. Adam, I am really disappointed. All the reports reaching me agree on one thing: There is no progress whatsoever. Crescendo, isn't that the name you gave him?"—I nodded—"has barely learnt anything."

"It depends on what you define as learning, Colonel Anthony. Crescendo has attained a lot in terms of personal development. He now trusts me as his best friend. This is a foundation to build on."

"Then, why did you ask for this meeting? You just said that he can't cope," was his reply.

He was starting to get on my nerves.

"Crescendo is not coping because of those same people sending you these reports. They are intimidating him. If it is up to me and him only, he would have learnt much more," I responded, furious.

With a sardonic smile, he replied, "Do you think we brought you here just to make friends with the giant? You are here for a mission, Mr. Adam. We want him to be a modern man with modern lifestyle, modern values, modern ethics, and modern attitude—and quickly!"

"I am wondering why Crescendo and myself are here. Why are we on this campus? Maybe he'd be more comfortable where he used to live." Before he objected, I added, "If where he used to live is now different due to oil exploration activities, we can send him to a similar place elsewhere."

Another sardonic smile from Anthony. "You are so naïve, Mr. Adam. Probably, you know already of my military background. There is a national, and possibly an international security, perspective to this story. If we don't adopt him, he'll fall in others' hands. Somebody already mentioned that he was heard speaking an uncanny language; perhaps Arabic or Chinese." I laughed. "He didn't. This is his own jargon."

It was pointless to carry on. The meeting was completely futile. Yet, I did not quit.

*****

Next morning, I went to the town center for few hours. On my return, I was flustered by the noise in the corridor to my room: extremely loud music.

Obviously, it was coming from Crescendo's room. I entered to find him dancing with Natalie to the loud music video showing on the TV. The guy was really happy and so was Natalie. They invited me to join, yelling, "Ada, come on!" I did not hold back. The atmosphere was electric. So, why not?

After it all ended, we sat down to catch our breath.

Natalie saw the question in my eyes, so she volunteered to answer: "They ordered the TV back to the room." So Anthony had started to act. I did not mind since Crescendo was happy. Perhaps, I had been wrong about the gadgets.

The sequence of events progressed very rapidly over the next couple of weeks. The TV was followed by a flood of other devices: a video games console, a mobile phone, a laptop. Crescendo started to welcome other staff to his room; staff who operated the entertainment for him. But he was still struggling to use the toilet and refused the shower. He would sit on the bed to watch the TV but moved back to the carpet at bedtime. My time with him was only spent on entertainment. On the plus side, I could use the technology to teach him far better and faster.

The most horrible sequela of all was the effect on my sleep. My hypersomnia was converted to insomnia.[2] The loudness originating

---

2   Insomnia is a sleep disorder in which you have trouble falling and/or staying asleep. The condition can be short-term or can last a long time. It may also come and go. Acute insomnia lasts from one night to a few weeks. Insomnia is chronic when it happens at least three nights a week for three months or more.

from my neighbor's room, his excitement day and night with the products of the gadgets, the unusual times to which our schedule together was shifted, and his calling on me as his "24/7 customer service agent" for technical support; all of this shattered my sleeping pattern.

But the worst was yet to come. Crescendo attempted to rape Natalie (probably, he had seen something explicit on TV that he wanted to imitate). Nobody had thought of the lad's sexual needs until that moment and there was no easy solution, bearing in mind his stature and strength. His weight gain was another issue with possible health ramifications.

After a couple of other violent incidents, all inspired by TV and video games, some censorship started. I tried to interfere with some regulations, but Anthony's men disallowed me. When I complained about my insomnia, I was moved to a room in another building.

The week after, during my visit to Crescendo's room, he looked quite strange to me; very irritable, with red eyes and black circles around them. He could not remember anything he had learnt, and all of a sudden, he started hallucinating. I called the staff in charge and enquired, "For how long has Crescendo been continuously awake? This guy hasn't slept for days! You're killing him."

After I furiously knocked on doors and made more phone calls, help started to arrive, including medical personnel.

I was evicted from the campus on Anthony's orders. However, I would not betray Crescendo. I started to approach the media. It was not that difficult to make a buzz. News of the giant was vivid in the recent memory of the whole world. The media was still craving interesting updates.

Soon, activists kicked in and protests started. The pressure was mounting on Anthony and his gang. Things were progressing in the right direction for the first time and for that I was grateful.

Then, last night at 11 PM, when I was preparing to go to bed, I was astounded by the ring of the doorbell. Had Anthony sent somebody to get rid of me? I've never been a fan of conspiracy theories, but it was a very reasonable apprehension given the context. Clutching my handgun, I advanced toward the door on my tiptoes, looked through the peephole...to my astonishment, it was Natalie!

Cautiously, I opened the door. I hoped Crescendo hadn't done it again.

She looked around quickly and swiftly entered, closing the door behind her.

"Natalie. What a surprise!! What happened? I mean, you are welcome. Come and sit down," I blathered.

After settling, Natalie explained to me that we needed to act at once; Crescendo was endangered.

"I thought it was the other way round, with the latest developments."

She corrected me. "It was supposed to be, but Anthony and those behind him wouldn't accept that outcome. They are planning to move Crescendo at first light in the morning."

"Move him??!! Where??!!"

"I don't know. But we have to be ahead of them. We need to save him away from them instantly!"

"You must be kidding, Natalie. Us—a cleaner and a teacher—are meant to move a 2.3 meter tall giant out of a semi-military campus overnight without any preparation or help?!!"

"There are arrangements and help." When she saw the bafflement in my eyes, she added: "Trust me. There are."

I looked into her eyes and I believed it was not a trap.

The next hour proved that Natalie was not on her own. A car awaited us outside my house and transported us to the campus. There, we used complicated routes that I'd never used before. There were actually a bunch of staff to help all through. Who was they loyal to? Who led them? Even now, I am not certain.

Eventually, I reached Crescendo's room. He was sitting on his bed with the same red eyes encircled by black rings. His face was unprecedently drained. The TV was on maximum volume, probably set that way by somebody else on this occasion.

"Ada." He looked at me with a longing look and pronounced the word more softly than I'd ever heard from him.

After a brief hug, we moved back through the campus along the same route. Natalie waved us goodbye at the exit.

Before leaving her behind, I looked at her gratefully and said, "I am glad you forgave him."

"I was never appalled by him." She grinned.

I walked for a few steps then returned to her again and added, "You're not actually a cleaner, are you?"

After a couple of seconds, she smiled: "I am indeed."

In the vehicle, we had three people with us. I looked around through the windows to the woods surrounding the road as it crested the hill. I learnt that we were being taken to a city hotel, where Crescendo would stay to publicize his case, seeking the best care available. I wasn't sure he could bear such immense pressure on top of what he already had.

All of a sudden, we realized we were being chased! The vehicle behind us had started to speed closer and closer.

After a short period of chasing, an acute turn threw our vehicle off the motorway and into a wooded area. Nobody was hurt. I grabbed the chance, pulling Crescendo out of the vehicle and starting to run through the woods. Crescendo had never been so compliant with me. He did exactly what I wished he would do.

****

I am not sure for how long I napped before the reappearance of Crescendo. Kindly, he lifted me up on his shoulder like his own child. A couple of miles from where we separated, he took me to a cave he had found safe. He dropped me on a bed of straw; one of two he prepared for us. Then he went out again, probably to look for breakfast.

I am not sure how long we would be staying in this resort. Nonetheless, it was a much-needed opportunity for both of us to heal and recover.

Crescendo's straw bed for me was comfier than the seven-star bed on campus. I was so happy to have my hypersomnia back.

Welcome to Dreamland

- The changes our bodies experience on a 24-hour cycle in response to light and darkness are known as the circadian rhythm (the biological clock).

- Our biological clock consists of genes and proteins functioning in a feedback loop orchestrating mental, physical and behavioral changes.

- The "master clock" is a group of nerves in the brain called the suprachiasmatic nucleus (SCN). It contains about 20,000 cells. The SCN is located just above the optic nerves that relay information from the eyes to the brain.

- The SCN controls the production of melatonin, a hormone that makes you sleepy. The master clock receives information about incoming light from the eyes. When the environment gets darker, the SCN tells the brain to produce more melatonin so that you get drowsy.

- We need to keep our biological clock on track by maintaining a consistent sleep schedule. Going to bed and waking up at the same time every day even during weekends (with a maximum deviation of 30 minutes) supports the circadian rhythm.

- Natural sunlight turns certain internal processes on or off to initiate the daytime activity. Exposing yourself to as much light as possible switches off the production of melatonin.

- Computer, tablet, smartphone, and TV screens emit blue light, which interferes with circadian rhythms. It instructs the brain to stop making melatonin

References: 1-3.

TITUS' MAGIC SOLUTION

February 1699:

Both walked slowly to the doctor's room, Titus out of laziness and Arabella out of fatigue.

As they sat down, Titus started: We are still the same, Dr Arnop; she still sleeps too little.

Arabella: And he still sleeps too much.

Dr Arnop: Nothing worked? The rose petals, the lavender, the marjoram[3]??!!

Arabella: Nor the almond milk blended with barley.

Titus: Nor the flowers of borage[4] and violets in rose water sweetened with sugar.

Dr Arnop: Have you stopped drinking tea and coffee, Madame?

Arabella: Long ago.

Dr Arnop: Have you tried the chamomile flowers with the spirit?

---

3   An aromatic herb in the mint family that has been grown in the Mediterranean, North Africa, and Western Asia for thousands of years. While similar to oregano, it has a milder flavor.

4   Also known as starflower, bee bush, bee bread, and bugloss, a medicinal herb with edible leaves and flowers, a preferred hotspot for bees.

Arabella: Yes indeed.

Dr Arnop: Excuse me. Which spirit have you blended?

Titus: Just beer.

Dr Arnop had finally found a loophole!

Dr Arnop: Ah-ha! See! This is the problem. Blending with beer is not for you, Madame.

Arabella, disappointed: I heard it is good for healthy sleep, Doctor.

Dr Arnop: Not for the ladies, Madame. This is more for men. For women, I advise red wine.

Arabella: This is pricey!

Titus: What about me?

Dr Arnop: My prescription for you, Mr. Titus, will be slices of bread steeped in vinegar then applied to the soles of your feet. And for you, Madame, try please cold cucumber and lettuce on your head, neck and stomach at bedtime. I would recommend as well to dip a cloth in milk mixed with red rose leaves and a slice of nutmeg then wipe your bed with it at sleep time—

Titus (interrupting):—But wouldn't this make me even more sleepy, as we sleep on the same bed?

Dr Arnop: Of course, of course. She should rub it on her side of the bed only. Be optimistic, please. This is the most important of all. Spring is approaching and it will help healing all your sleep issues.

***

April 1699:

She made sure the wolves' teeth bands were surrounding the necks of her small angels and the carved knives were hung above their cradles as usual; children should be protected at all times from the evil of nightmares. Then, Arabella turned to her own bed. Titus was deeply asleep as usual. She started putting the warm stones between the bed sheets, then she hung the cow dung at the foot of the bed. She is used now to the smell and Titus would never be woken up by any smell whatsoever. The dung smell is bearable, but the fleas, flies, and bugs are not.

She lay on her right side, as advised by Dr Arnop, to ease the passage of dinner through the stomach. One hour, two hours passed and no sleep. She turned to her left side, as advised by Dr Arnop, to pass the gases to the other side and distribute the heat evenly on both sides, but no luck.

Nothing this doctor advised is helping. Her all-time drunk husband is sleeping even more after the doctor's white wine advice. She will go tomorrow to Honoria, the wise woman. Her friend Vecula has tried her before with success.

Next morning, having slept for only a couple of hours, tired as usual Arabella is accompanied by her friend Vecula on her way to Honoria's hut.

"Do you sleep with your mouth open or closed dear, Arabella?" Honoria asked.

"I don't know. I don't remember, to be honest."

"Ah. This is an issue, my dear. You should keep your mouth open whilst asleep, to keep your chimneys clear of foul humors," Honoria added.

"Foul humors?!!"

"Yes, indeed; your phlegm, blood, yellow bile and black bile. Your doctor never told you that?!!"

"Never!!"

"Shame on him!! Doctors are not as good nowadays," a disappointed Honoria commented.

"So, that's it?! Keep my mouth open?"

"Yes. And what about your man who sleeps too much?" asked Honoria. "What does he do for a living?"

"He is a carpenter, but there's not enough work for him to do. So, he sleeps night and day," Arabella replied.

"He needs more work then. Listen, I have connections with Count Quartus' palace. I'll find him some work. Don't worry."

※

June 1699:

As per the scheduled appointment following Sunday service, Titus knocked on priest Lancelot's door.

The priest asked him, "Are you still sleeping too much, unfortunate Titus?"

"Yes, father."

"But I heard you are now working in the palace."

"True father. But then again, count Quartus is sick all the time. Everybody is busy with him and I sleep sitting there with no job to do."

The priest asked about Titus' spouse: "She still can't sleep well?"

"She keeps on trying to keep her mouth open all night long, hanging things on her lips, sticking stuff in between, and making these horrible sounds with no blessing."

"What time do both of you wake up in the morning?"

"I wake up at noon. I find her always awake. I never see her sleeping," Titus responded.

"You have to force yourself to rise with the sun, my son. With the early morning shine, a series of irresistible events open your body pores, pushing the spirits outwards, getting the heat and blood to surface from the innermost areas deep inside your body."

"Right."

Father Lancelot asked: "And do you do your bedtime prayers with your family before both sleeps[5]?"

---

5   Until the invention of artificial light, people—especially in cold counties—used to segment their night sleep into two parts, four hours each; the first starts with sunset, followed by two hours of waking for some chat, entertainment, sex, prayers, and meditation, "depending on the local culture", then the second part. In warmer countries, a siesta would be a different option, when people nap during the hot hours of afternoon.

"Second sleep usually, but we often miss it with the first."

The priest got closer to Titus. "Never ever miss a prayer," he instructed. "The Devil and his servants use those opportunities to possess and deform people, especially men."

"Especially men??!!"

Lancelot came even closer and whispered, "They deform penises."

A scared, astonished look ensued in Titus' eyes: "Really??!!!"

The priest nodded sadly. "Every few weeks, those miserable folks come here and sit in your exact place"—Titus stood up instantly—"devastated by the forfeiture of their masculinity and fertility. If not for the vow of clandestineness, I would tell you their names."

***

August 1699:

It was one of those lovely summer evenings, with a tranquil breeze wafting from the north. The four of them were having a long chat, with lots of giggles and plenty of amusement, sitting in the back garden: Arabella, Titus, Vecula, and her husband Barnaby, who just returned from a four-month journey to the east. As a sailor, Barnaby had many stories to tell, filling hours with tales about the diverse countries he had visited and the various people and cultures he had encountered.

At the end of the visit, Barnaby went inside the house and came out with gifts for his guests.

"Thank you, dear Barnaby. What are these?" asked Titus.

"Pajamas."

"Pajamas??!! They look to by very comfy. I would feel very cozy if I went to work in these garments." Titus felt the texture. "What are they made of? Linen, I presume?"

Barnaby explained. "Yes, made of linen. But these garments are not for going out, dear Titus. These are for sleep."

"Oooooooh," wondered Titus and Arabella in one breath.

"Just for sleep?" asked an amazed Arabella. "From where did you buy these japomas?" she asked.

"Pajamas," Barnaby corrected. Then he added, "From India. There, people wear them just for bedtime." He clarified more. "They don't wear them under their day clothes like we do with shifts. They take them off in the morning and put them on again at night."

"Wow!!! Do you think they will help me sleep deeper?" mused Arabella.

"Certainly. Especially if you take a warm bath beforehand, like they do in the east."

"We do that every month or so."

"They bath every day there," Barnaby clarified.

"Every *day*???!!!"

***

October 1699:

For the first few weeks, the daily bathing and the pajamas worked fine for Titus and Arabella's night slumber. Yet, as the weeks passed by, they got used to the feeling of the pajamas and they slowed down on the bathing habit; it was too exhausting to haul all of those heavy buckets of water and warm them up every evening.

Titus suggested seeing another doctor, but this was resented by Arabella, who complained, "They are no good. I don't want to see doctors any more, Titus."

"This is the palace doctor, Arabella. He is treating Count Quartus."

"And why on earth would Count Quartus' doctor agree to treat Count Quartus' carpenter?!!" Arabella questioned, surprised by the notion.

"Oh, Arabella. Please. Don't undervalue my aptitudes. I was backed by Rhoda, to be honest."

Now, Arabella is more upset than surprised. "Ah Rhooooda!!! The countess' maid? It seems you are getting along quite well."

"We are," responded Titus, but he added immediately, "as friends only. Please don't be jealous. Don't misjudge."

Since Arabella mulishly insisted she would not go, Titus went on his own to see Dr Septimus.

After finishing the examination, the doctor told him, "Titus, I believe you have some reflux[6]."

"And why is that making me sleep more, Doctor?"

Dr Septimus explained: "Your sleep is often disrupted all through the night, Titus. You are not conscious of it when asleep. Then, you make up for it with daytime sleep."

"And how should I manage this, Doctor?"

"Well. You need to slumber well-bolstered up, with your head raised and a downward slope towards your stomach. Also, before bedtime, take your dairy lid posset; that's a lettuce soup that should be soporific."

∗∗∗

December 1699:

This Christmas season, Arabella has never been happier. The family's nights are much more settled. She now believes in medicine. Dr Septimus' treatment has done wonders for herself and her husband. Every night, Titus prepares this dairy lid posset for both of them. He sleeps well-bolstered up and she sticks some small bags of aniseed to her nostrils, then both of them doze as deeply and peacefully as a dreaming baby. He rises early for work. When she wakes up in the morning, he is not there. Titus is currently less interested in having sex with her, but possibly this is a transition period. She'll be patient with him.

---

6   A condition where the contents of the stomach regurgitate up to the gullet causing heart burn and possible sleep disruption.

But the appeasing nights unfortunately did not last for long. One night, Arabella felt full. She did not want to drink the posset. Exhausted Titus was asleep already, but she could not. She tried to stick the aniseed bags in her nose further, but they did not work. Desperately, she brought two more bags and pushed them in. Yet, the slumber she had enjoyed over the past few weeks was elusive.

Half asleep, a couple of hours later, Arabella felt Titus sneaking out of bed. "It's too early for work," she thought. She did not move. Titus started preparing to go out. It was obvious he was being extremely wary with his movements so as not to produce the slightest din. This was not the Titus she had known for 12 years. This man had a secret.

The next night, Arabella decided on a trick. She managed to stealthily swap her posset with Titus'. He did not notice. On that night, the doze did not approach Arabella's eyes like the previous night and the old nights, whereas Titus slept like a log. She even tried hard to shake him awake, but he was a rock.

So, Titus was spiking her posset with something to make her sleep deeply without telling her. He must be having an affair. With whom? Rhoda the palace maid, she is pretty sure.

The night after, Arabella did not swap the possets, but she managed to spill hers away furtively. In the middle of the night, Titus got up, sneaking again, but this time Arabella started covertly following him at a distance.

As she expected, Titus was heading to the palace. Her suspicions grew further when she saw him covering his face, whilst he clandestinely entered the palace through a hidden back entrance rather than the main gate or the servants' door, which were both securely locked. She could see from distance a woman opening the door for him. Arabella was too far away to distinguish her features, but she figured it must be Rhoda. Titus went in. Arabella waited and waited.

He was clearly not coming out again. There was no way for her to enter; it was pointless to stay. So, she returned home.

As Titus came back in the evening, Arabella had her own special welcome for him. It was the most delicious dinner he'd had all year, with all the food he adores—the hashed chicken with turnip and roast quinces, the verjuice, and treacle tart. The most imperative ingredient was the pills she had found in his pocket. These were dissolved in his verjuice. Arabella has put them all in, not omitting a single pill. They had been stolen by Rhoda earlier from Count Quartus' medicine cabinet. Dr Septimus had been using them regularly to help the count overcome his pains with a long deep sleep.

Later, Vecula has been waiting for hours in her pajamas, looking from her balcony every now and then, but the man she awaits has not shown up. She has been feeling abandoned by her sailor husband Barnaby who has been away for a couple of months so far, and now it seems that she is getting dumped by her lover as well! Titus will not wake up any time soon, not in her lifetime.

The Ancient World and Dreamland

- 8,000 BCE: Ancient circular sleeping abodes resembling birds' nests, signifying that the fetal position was most favored in this era, have been revealed by archeologists.

- 1,300 BCE: Bed frames with stuffed mattresses started to become popular. Straw was the first material to be used.

- 800 BCE: The ancient Egyptians built temples to worship the goddess Isis, where priests gathered to interpret dreams.

- The Greeks viewed sleep as a middle state between life and death. In Greek mythology, Hypnos (the god of sleep) and Thanatos (the god of death) were the children of Nyx (the goddess of night).

- 400-500 BCE: Aristotle suggested that sleep is "a seizure of the primary sense-organ, rendering it unable to actualize its powers, arising of necessity ... for the sake of its conservation." The seizure part was imprecise, but the conservation part was correct, as explained by modern sleep science.

- The earliest references to segmented sleep were written in The Odyssey, in which Homer mentions the "first sleep." The interval between the two parts of sleep was an opportunity for people to socialize, enjoy entertainment, relax, or have sex. This practice continued until the invention of artificial lighting and its growing prevalence in the 19th century.

- All of the sleep recipes mentioned in "Titus' magic solution" are real 17th-century practices, but the story itself is fictional.

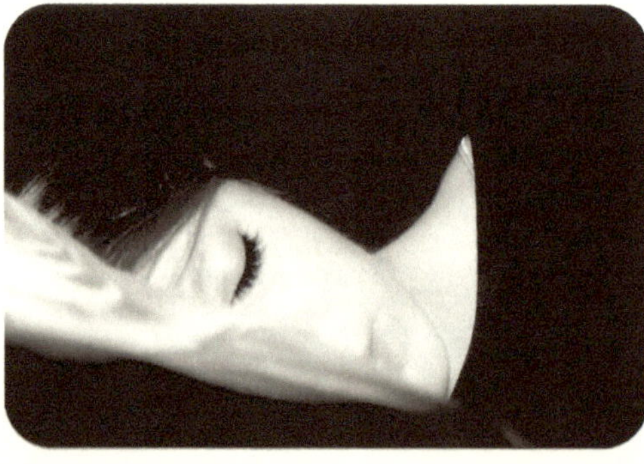

References: 4-6.

HARD TIMES

He is a legendary author who created some of the most vivid characters the world of literature has ever known, the greatest writer of the Victorian era. Yet, within the context of this book, Charles Dickens had an underrated talent on which he is also second to none. Dickens is the best fiction author ever when it comes to describing the sleep difficulties of his characters.

This aspect of Dickens' writings has an important background in the genius author's own struggle with sleep disruption for many years. Dickens never opened up about the cause of his sleep disruption, but many believe that it was related to the internal conflict between his love for the 27-years-younger actress Nelly Ternan and his 20-year marriage to Catherine Hogarth, and his severe anxiety of a subsequent scandal that resulted. Yet, more recently, it was revealed that Dickens had a bipolar psychiatric disorder[7] with alternating mood changes between depression and mania[8]. Interestingly, Dickens would suffer from depression at the beginning of writing a novel and get mania closer to the end of his work. Several academics contemplate that the psychiatric disorder and the related excessive mood swings were at least partially accountable for Dickens' insomnia.

Several of Dickens' supreme novels were written during his insomnia era, including: *Bleak House, Hard Times, Little Dorrit and A Tale of Two Cities.*

---

7   A mental disorder characterized by periods of depression and periods of abnormally elevated mood that last from days to weeks each.

8   A state of abnormally elevated arousal, affect, and energy level.

Night walks

Dickens had his own way to overcome his suffering, which he described himself: "Some years ago, a temporary inability to sleep, caused me to walk about the streets all night. I would get up directly after lying down, go out, and come home tired at sunrise. My principal object to get through the night." Those walks would continue from after midnight until sunrise; more than 30 miles walks extending over seven hours on some occasions.

Charles Dickens wrote an eight-essay collection, *Night Walks,* reflecting on London's night life in the 1850s during his sleep-deprived strolls. He exposed homelessness, drunkenness and depravity on the streets. These superb articles showcased the crime and corruption, the ventures of chasing fortune, the awkward wrongdoers, the huge marine business, the miserable working and living conditions, the fervent lottery seekers and the fraud abusing their ambitions and other aspects of the lively British social scenes in the mid-19th century.

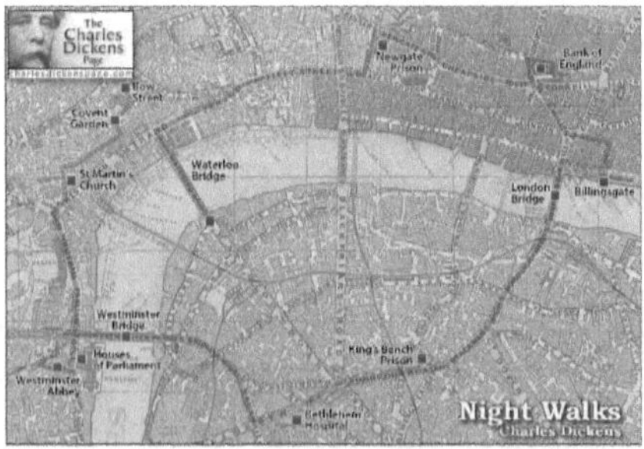

Bethlehem Psychiatric Hospital—a pioneer of its kind globally, as it is nearly 700 years old—drew some special attention amidst Dickens' night walks. He compared the residents inside with people outside, especially at sleep time, writing:

"Are not the sane and the insane equal at night as the sane lie a dreaming? Are not all of us outside this hospital, who dream, more or less in the condition of those inside it, every night of our lives? Are we not nightly persuaded that we associate with kings and queens, emperors and empresses? Do we not jumble events, people, times and places, as they do? One afflicted man said to me: Sir, I can frequently fly. I was half ashamed to reflect that so could I by night."

My favorite novelist would often finish his sleepless night by visiting a train station to observe the arrival of the morning mail:

"The station lamps would burst out ablaze. The porters would emerge, the cabs and trucks would rattle to their places, and, finally, the bell would strike up, and the train would come banging in, knowing that sunrise was not too far away."

These were signals denoting that the fatigued Dickens should go home for rest.

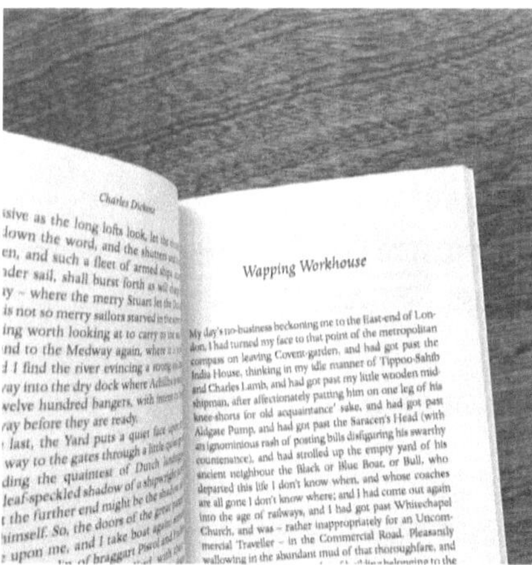

Pictures of sleep and its disorders in Dickens' literature

Back in 1992, *Sleep,* the journal of the American Sleep Disorders Association and Sleep Research Society, published an interesting article in which the author, J. E. Cosnett from the Neurology Unit, University of Natal, Durban, South Africa, reviewed examples of Dickens' descriptions of sleep and its disorders, as follows:

Insomnia in The Pickwick Papers: "Everyone has experienced that disagreeable state of mind, in which a sensation of bodily weariness in vain contends against an inability to sleep". Mr. Pickwick "tossed first on one side and then on the other; and perseveringly closed his eyes as if to coax himself to slumber". On this instance, his sleep was barred by "thoughts of grim pictures, and the stories to which they had given rise. He came to the conclusion that it was of no use trying to sleep, so he got up and ... dressed himself".

Insomnia in Dombey and son: Edith Granger finds "no rest in the tumult of her agitation. Thus, in the dead time of the night before her bridal, she wrestled with her unquiet spirit ...". Another character from the same script, Florence Dombey, allows personal relationships to disturb her sleep: "Her repugnance to this man ... invaded her dreams and disturbed the whole night. Rising in the morning, unrefreshed, and with a heavy recollection of the domestic unhappiness of the previous day." A third character, James Carker, in flight from Dombey, suffers from the same condition: "His object was to rest ... He was stupefied and he was wearied to death ... his drowsy senses would not lose their consciousness. He had no more influence with them in this regard, than if they had been another man's."

Parasomnias[9] have significant roles in Dickens' stories.

9　A category of sleep disorders involving abnormal movements, behaviors, emotions, perceptions, and dreams that occur while falling asleep, sleeping, between sleep stages, or during arousal from sleep.

He wrote about himself in the *Uncommercial traveler:* "It is a curiosity of broken sleep that I made immense quantities of verses ... and that I spoke a certain language, once familiar to me, but which I have nearly forgotten from disuse, with fluency. Of both these phenomena I have such frequent experience in the state between sleeping and waking, that I sometimes argue with myself that I know I cannot be awake ...".

The title character in *David Copperfield* pictures his sensations on attempting to keep awake: "I was dead sleepy ... I had reached that stage of sleepiness when Peggotty seemed to swell up and grow immensely large. I propped my eyelids open with my two forefingers ...".

Barnaby Rudge has hallucinations: " ... I have been asleep. There have been great faces coming and going-close to my face and then a mile away-low places to creep through—high churches to fall down from—strange creatures crowded up together neck and heels, to sit upon the bed ...".

In *Oliver Twist:* "Oliver ... was not thoroughly awake. There is a drowsy state, between sleeping and waking, when you dream more in five minutes with your eyes half open, and yourself half conscious of everything that is passing around you, than you would in five nights with your eyes fast closed, and your senses wrapt in perfect unconsciousness ... Oliver was in this condition ...".

The Victorian author was also knowledgeable regarding the phenomenon of sleep paralysis, as explained by Oliver's state in this passage: "There is a kind of sleep that steals upon us sometimes, which, while it holds the body prisoner, does not free the mind from a sense of things about it, and enable it to ramble at its pleasure. So far as an overpowering heaviness, a prostration of strength, and an utter inability to control our thoughts or power of motion, can be called sleep, this is it; and yet we have consciousness of all that is going on about us, and, if we dream at such a time, words which are really spoken, or sounds which really exist at the moment, accommodate themselves with surprising readiness to our visions, until reality and imagination become so strangely blended that it is afterwards almost a matter of impossibility to separate the two ...". The American physician Silas Weir Mitchell was the first to describe sleep paralysis on an academic basis in 1876, nearly 40 years after the publication of *Oliver Twist*.

Hypersomnia has been also featured in at least three of Dicken's novels:

Joe, the obese boy, on whom the Pickwickian syndrome was established, is introduced in *The Pickwick Papers* as " ... a fat and red-faced boy, in a state of somnolency".

William Dorrit in *Little Dorrit* dozes on inappropriate occasions, including one incident when " ... as he stood ... he fell into a heavy doze, of not a minute's duration, and awoke with a start".

In *Bleak House*, Hugh, the ostler at the Maypole Inn, is used to sleep on the job. One guest comments: "I should think if he were living, he would have heard you by this time". His employer replies: "In his fits of laziness, he sleeps so desperate hard ... that if you were to fire off cannon-balls into his ears, it wouldn't wake him".

The article proceeds to elaborate on numerous other examples from Dickens' writings related to sleep, both its normality and abnormalities.

The Dickensian solution

After exhausting the night walks solution, Charles Dickens tried drugs; he mixed opium with alcohol. Yet, this option caused him a horrendous hangover.

Dickens' daughter, Mary, who was an author herself, tells us how her father managed in the end to solve his sleep disorder: "He could be a fidget ... with regard to the furniture of a room in a hotel at which he might be spending only a single night, rearranging it all and turning the bed north and south to suit the requirements of the electrical currents of the earth."

Not only did Dickens believe that he should sleep with his head pointing north, he also had to lie precisely in the middle of the bed. He would spread his arms sideways and fidget until he satisfied his obsession with his body being in the exact center.

References: 7-10.

Famous People and Bizarre Dreamland Habits

- Vincent Van Gogh, the Dutch painter, managed his insomnia by dousing his mattress and pillow with camphor, which gradually intoxicated him and lead to his suicide.

- Emily Bronte, the British author, treated her insomnia with night walks like Dickens but not around London streets—only around her dining table until she fell asleep.

- Napoleon Bonaparte, the French leader, used to have a total daily sleep of four interrupted hours, from 00:00 – 02:00 and from 05:00 – 07:00.

- Tom Cruise, the American actor, sleeps in a sound-proof, small, dark and comfortable snoratorium, so that his loud snoring is not heard outside when the door is locked.

- Nicola Tesla, the Croatian inventor, used to have terrible nightmares as a child. So, he followed what is known as Uberman sleep: six cycles of 20 minutes sleep with a total of two hours sleep per 24 hours. He once worked 84 hours without rest. Thomas Edison and Leonardo Da Vinci, the American and Italian inventors, respectively, used to do the same but with some variations in timing.

- Mariah Carey, the American singer, sleeps for more than 60% of the day (15 hours) and wakes up only for nine hours. She has 20 humidifiers around her bed to transform it into a steam room.

- Michael Phelps, the American swimmer, sleeps in a chamber with an atmosphere equivalent to 9,000 feet altitude to force the production of more red blood cells by his body for more oxygen delivery to his muscles.

References: *11-12.*

ANOTHER HORRIBLE
TUESDAY

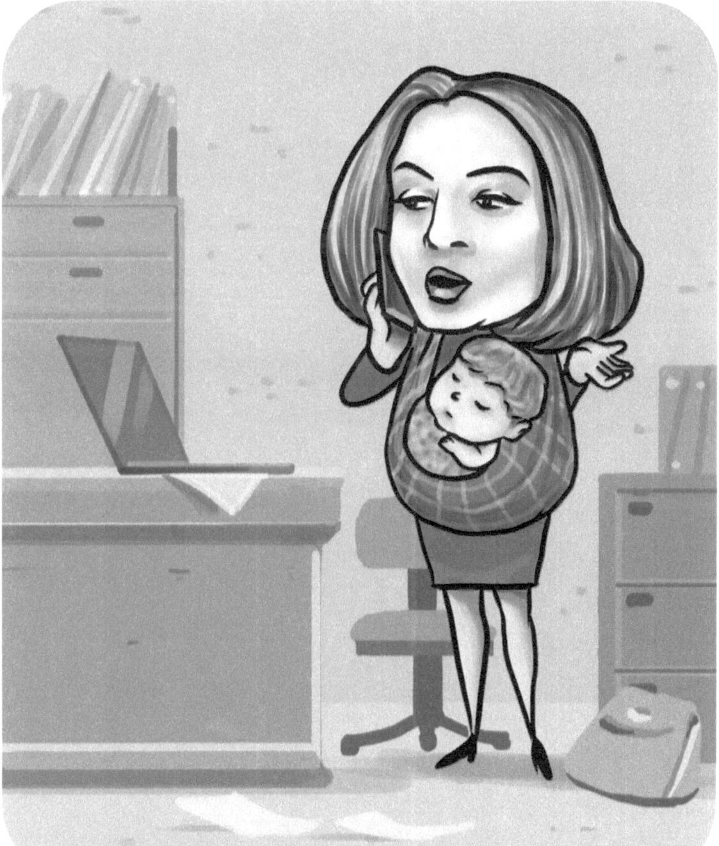

"Dear diary...

Oh, no—

Dear *awful* diary. It is another horrid Tuesday. First thing in the morning, I rushed into Jane's office, struggling to hold my tears back. As usual, she barely glanced at me from above her specs with her typical stony look:

"What's up?"

The way she asked enraged me even more.

Fuming, I said, "You very well know what's up, Jane. Clark has taken the GM[10] position!" With an untouched tone she replied, "You were aware it had been going this way for long time, Lisa."

After a deep breath to dilute my anger in an attempt at self-control, I responded, "No. I wasn't. By what standard had this been obvious? I'm older than him, have been here longer, have higher qualifications, more experience, work harder and—"

"—And you had a tiff with the COO[11] last month," she interrupted, not forgetting her callous smile.

---

10 General manager.

11 Chief operating officer.

"Yeah. That bastard."

"The COO can't be a bastard."

"Well. I didn't know he was the COO!"

"Darling. Every middle-aged well-dressed man in the company's anniversary reception is a potential COO."

I hate Jane even more when she spits out these grandma's pearls of wisdom.

I suddenly felt tired. I sat down opposite her.

"Didn't you see how he was sitting, spreading his legs, encroaching on my personal space even with his extended arms??!!"

Again, the callous smile and the deadpan answer: "Lisa. That's just how men sit."

"I don't have to accept that," I said. Then, pointing at her, I added, "*You* shouldn't accept that. *We* should change that."

"Lisa. Here, we don't change. We adapt. Evolution. Survival of the fittest. We do what those above us do."

"Spread our legs??!!"

A moment of awkwardness followed that outburst.

Jane tried to rectify her words. "That's not what I meant. Let me be frank with you, Lisa. You are too feminine to be a boss. A typical

Generation X[12] lady. The company will never offer leadership opportunities to your sort of personality.”

“Oh, come on! You’re Generation X yourself and you’re no.3 from the top.”

“I’m different.”

That was my chance to bite: “A bit masculine, you mean?”

I knew it hit the heart of the target, but she absorbed it. To be honest, she is pretty good like that. “Well,” she replied, “I gave up a lot of things, and this is exactly my point. You can’t be the business mogul, the sexy lady turning heads, the awesome wife and the terrific mother. Forget about the 24-hour woman of Enjoli[13].” Her sarcastic body language emanated all over the office.

Oh my God! This woman is a cocktail of envy and jealousy.

“Jane. What’s Clark’s performance score this year?”

“It’s not just about one single figure, Lisa. You’re aware it’s more complex than that. But yes, yours was better.”

“See!”

It seemed to be a triumph ... just for few seconds, until she found some logic for her rebuttal.

---

12 Generation X includes people born between the years 1965 and 1980. Women of this generation were raised with an aim of having it all; being successful business women, wonderful wives and amazing mothers. The immense difficulties for achieving such superwoman state posed huge pressure on this generation.

13 A Enjoli perfume commercial in the 80s propagated the image of a 24-hour woman capable of doing everything in perfection at work and home.

"You are far better, Lisa. Technically. Yet, he has far better connections and communications, precisely what we need for a GM position. Who got us the Minerva deal? Clark. Who got us the Plutona deal? It was Clark. Who settled our dispute with the department of Energy? You guessed it. And that night when you fell out with the COO, do you know what Clark was doing? He was having a hilarious chat with the CEO for over half an hour!"

This was beyond my tolerance. This was beyond the pale. I left her and rushed to the door. Yet, she couldn't pass up this opportunity to get on my nerves.

"—And Clark doesn't nap at work!"

"NAAAAAAP?!!!!! NAAAAAAAAP?!!! NAAAAAAAAAAAP?!!!!!!" The words echoed through my mind. I was incensed.

Hastily, I returned, all guns blazing again.

"Are you, by any tiny trivial minute chance, hinting that I *doze* at work?"

"I'm not hinting. I'm telling you frankly that you *do* doze, you *do* nap at work. Everybody is talking and joking about it".

There was nothing to say really. No comment could have silenced nasty Jane. No words could adequately portray her insolence.

She was probably referring to yesterday's meeting when I had dozed for a few seconds then asked the same question answered a minute earlier.

But so what?

This happens all the time. People often slumber during those boring meetings.

I only nap in the office when I am extremely tired, which doesn't happen on a daily basis.

Napping while driving? Well, that would be a major problem if it caused accidents, not just one minor crash.

And napping in front of TV is the norm ...

I can't focus anymore at the moment. That's enough for tonight.

Oh. It's already 4 AM.

Excuse me, diary. I'll have to go now.

My fifth attempt at sleep.

Wish me luck, please.

Oh, and sorry for my rudeness earlier.

Lisa Bernard
21/10/2020

Lisa Bernard is definitely not alone. She is not by any means an odd case of a middle-aged working woman struggling with stress and anxiety and experiencing sleep disturbances both as a cause and a consequence.

The March/April 2014 issue of *Bethesda Magazine,* a district journal for a well-to-do area of Washington, D.C., was at the time of publication very popular for a profile of Melissa "Missy" Lesmes, "a veritable supermom." The article stated:

"A fit, petite, vivacious blonde, Missy is at age 46 a wife, a mother of four kids ranging in age from 11 to 18 and all in separate schools, a partner at a prestigious Washington, D.C. law firm … a party maven always up for a gathering at her Chevy Chase home, a longtime friend to women who profess she's always there when they need her, and a woman who still manages to give back to the community."

The profile was published under the title "We Don't Know How She Does It."

Missy's daily schedule was outlined by the magazine:

"Missy rises at 5:30 AM to run on the Capital Crescent Trail or head downtown to work out with a personal trainer. She's back home by 7 AM to make sure the kids are awake and getting ready for school."

... "Arrives at her spacious office by 8:30 or so"

... "gets home between 7:30 and 8"

Dinner whilst standing up, homework help, and bed for the kids at "10 or 10:30", sleeps at midnight.

In her interview with *Bethesda Magazine*, Lesmes said that it had all started when she was at college. "That was the point I realized I wanted to keep busy," she said. "Once I started down that road, I started to realize I like having [money], so that motivated me a lot as well." Yet, it seems she will never feel satisfied: "I can't be the perfect mom. I want to be, but there's just not enough time, not enough hours."

A role model to follow, was the conclusion.

Actually, a 60% majority of Generation X working women describe themselves as stressed about essential issues like their finances and caring for their families. Half of those sleep less than seven hours per night on average.

A 2016 Gallup poll revealed that 16% of Generation X were single and had never been married between the ages of 18 and 30, compared to 10% of Boomers[14] and just 4% of their grandparents' generation. This is more typical of women who achieved higher education and sought higher positions at work. According to the Pew Research

---

14   The Boomer Generation is generally defined as people born from 1946 to 1964, during the post–World War II baby boom.

Center, about 25% of perimenopausal women with at least a master's degree have never had children.

You may presume that these women must be doing well financially then. Unfortunately, Generation X has run into debts and is saving less than any other generation. This is true for women more than men, without even getting into inequality caused by the gender pay.

So, it is a cycle of stress, anxiety and insomnia, boosting one another in a vicious cycle.

If depression kicks in, the cycle turns into a ticking, life-threatening bomb just waiting to go off.

References: 13-16.

Women, Stress, and Dreamland

- From puberty until the age of 50, a woman is twice as likely to have an anxiety disorder as a man. Women are more sensitive to low levels of corticotropin-releasing factor (CRF), a hormone that organizes stress responses in mammals, augmenting their liability to stress-related conditions.

- Women are also more likely to have multiple psychiatric disorders during their lifetime than men.

- The brain system involved in the fight-or-flight response is activated more readily in women and stays activated longer, partly due to the action of estrogen and progesterone (female hormones).

- Women need about 20 more minutes of sleep than men do due to multitasking and slightly more consumption of brain energy.

- A 2005 Sleep in America poll revealed that women are more likely than men to have difficulty falling and staying asleep and to experience more daytime drowsiness at least a few nights/days a week.

- A recent study concluded that overweight, post-menopausal women exercising in the morning fall asleep easier and better than evening exercisers.

- 58% of women suffer from nighttime pain (compared to 48% of men), according to a 1996 Gallup Poll. In a 2000 Sleep in America poll, 25% of women reported sleep interruption due to pain or physical discomfort three nights a week or more.

- One large study of female night shifts workers over a three-year period found they were of a 60% higher risk for developing breast cancer. In 2009, the Danish government starting paying compensations to the victims based on this study.

References: 17-22.

DEATH BY POVERTY OF TIME[15]

"September, 2014

Pleasanton, USA

I came back to the US to be with my family again. My dear son was now a proud member of Goldman Sachs. Immediately, I rushed to see him in San Francisco.

I vividly remember him walking towards me, outside his majestic office. It is difficult to narrate the barrage of emotions that swept my heart as he approached me. I hugged him strongly, not letting him go for few minutes. He touched my face and tears rolled down our cheeks.

What can I do to get back that moment again in this life? Why does life give such precious and memorable moments, which cannot even be retained in your heart?

It is unfair, unjust, and unfathomable.

We went for a coffee and pizza. There was so much to hear from him. His experiences, his associates, his feelings and job satisfaction. Obviously, he was happy and excited. During the flow of intense conversation, we ate garlic bread, assuming it to be the main course pizza. We laughed heartily at our stupidity when the waiter brought a sumptuous pizza after we had pigged out on the complementary garlic bread. It was great fun. After the meal, my son offered to pay the check. My chest swelled with pride. My emotions were uncontrollable. My eyes were moist with love, pride, and happiness.

Now that he is working, he could come to Pleasanton only on weekends. Even when he came, he was tired and sleepy.

"Papa, I do not get enough sleep. I work twenty hours at a stretch." During certain weeks, he was working on weekends too.

I protested, "Son, you will ruin your health."

He replied, 'Come on, Papa, I am young and strong. Investment banking is hard work.'

I could not say anything beyond this, but obviously, my wife and I were not pleased with the scheme of things.

Autumn was not turning out to be as good as summer. He had less time, was mentally and physically fatigued and above all, without sleep. However, we made the best of the time available to us. We did go for our walks, a little cycling, and occasionally to the gym.

On my last day, he could not come to see me, he was busy. So, I went to meet him in San Francisco. We drank coffee and with heavy hearts, bid adieu. I still remember him, waving to me as I went down to the underground Bart station.

An image ... that is all I am left with.

Nothing can give me peace now, no one can return my moments of bliss, nowhere can I find peace, never will I be that spirited again.

Is there really an order in the nature of things? Surely, there must be. How else can we explain day and night, change of seasons, growing up?

So, where does the order go when nature has to play its game of keeping balance of life on this planet? Can we have spring before winters or summer after autumn? So, why to disturb the order of age? Why is the supernatural so whimsical? Why so heartless? Why irrational?

I know, no one will ever answer my questions.

Beginning of the End

Spring, 2015

San Francisco

The New Year began modestly and silently. It gave no indication that it was carrying in its womb, a catastrophe, a calamity, which no parent can envisage in their life time.

My heartbeat, my son, was settling down well in his job. His phone calls were far and few, as he was extremely busy, but emails and messages were keeping the lifeline working.

From mid-January, he started complaining. "This job is not for me. Too much work and too little time. I want to come back home."

As probably any parent would react, we counselled him to keep going, as such difficult phases were inevitable in a high-pressure new job. "Sonny, all of your age, young and ambitious, feel like this. Keep going," I would say.

Gradually, his complaints and his discomfort with his job increased in intensity and frequency. In our emails, messages, and phone calls, we continued to empathize with him, but we did not give him an open mandate to quit, as he probably wanted.

In the third week of March 2015, he submitted his resignation, without consulting us, and called us. My first sentence to him was, "Sonny I did not want you to quit, but now since you have done so, we are with you. Come back home."

He sounded sad and disturbed, saying, "Papa, it will take some time for me to leave. HR will take some time to clear my resignation.'

I asked, "What you want to do now?"

"Well, I will rejuvenate myself, eat home-cooked food, walk and go to gym, and finally work with and expand our school," he replied.

This was not something I wanted him to do, at this stage of his career. I desired that he should complete his one year at Goldman Sachs, learn something about corporate life, and then decide.

Destiny was marking its time for the family. We had no clue that we were going to be hit by a tsunami, which would uproot our lives, never to be rooted again. By a quirk of fate, he was asked by his company to reconsider his resignation. Under pressure from me, he rejoined.

Now, I, who had nurtured him, carved him, possessed him, took the fatal decision for him. Why did I ask him to continue? Why didn't I ask him to come back? What if I had not forced him to stay? What if his company had not given him the window to reconsider his resignation?

These painful questions will never be answered. There is no power in this universe that can undo the tragedy that hit us.

Poor son, he rejoined and did his best to come to terms with the hard, continuous work, with no breaks, no sleep, and no respite.

April 16, 2015, 2:40 AM, California time. He calls us and says, "It is too much. I have not slept for two days, have a client meeting tomorrow morning, have to complete a presentation, my VP is annoyed, and I am working alone in my office."

I got furious. "Take fifteen days leave and come home immediately," I said.

He blurted, "They will not allow that".

"Then tell them to consider this as your resignation letter," was my response.

Finally, he agreed to complete his work in about an hour, go to his apartment, which was half a mile from his office block, and return in the morning."[16]

✳✳✳

But Sonny never returned in the morning. Exactly 90 minutes after this conversation, he jumped to his demise from the balcony of his apartment. His lifeless body was found in the parking lot at 06:40 AM local time.

The excerpt above from a letter written by Sarvshreshth Gupta's father was at the heart of hard talk within business circles during the summer of 2015. The incident was not by any means the first or the last of its kind:

- Ilya Zhitomirskiy, co-founder and developer of the Diaspora social network and the Diaspora free software that powers it was found dead in his San Francisco home. An autopsy report from the Medical Examiner's office formally ruled the death as a suicide. He died from an intentional inert gas asphyxiation using helium. Zhitomirskiy's mother Inna did say on his participation in Diaspora, "I strongly believe that if Ilya did not start this project and stayed in school, he would be well and alive today."

---

16   An account from Mr. Sunil Gupta on his son's death, published for the first time in The New York Times and on Medium on the June 2, 2015 (Later removed, but it had already spread to other media in USA, UK & India), edited for this book.

- In August 2013, Bank of America intern Moritz Erhardt died after reportedly working consecutive all-nighters at the bank's London office.

- In 2014, a series of deaths of employees stationed in JP Morgan Chase's Hong Kong branch and London headquarters resulted in bankers fearing for their own lives.

- Six weeks after Gupta's suicide, Thomas Hughes, a 29-year-old Moelis & Co. banker, was found dead outside his residence in New York, where he lived on the 24th floor. His injuries were consistent with a fall, police said. His father told *The Daily Mail* that his son didn't have much free time from work and that "at a time when he was under stress he probably resorted to illegal drugs, causing this incredibly poor judgement."

- Encyclopedia Britannica's COO Vineet Whig, 47, killed himself in 2016 by jumping within a deep shaft of the building where he lived in Gurugram. His suicide note said, "I am taking my own life, no one is responsible. I am unable to cope. I am sorry. I am depressed. I see no way out except for suicide. Yes, I am a coward. I should have faced life."

Corporates have been trying to combat the enormous work load pressures on their employees for a decade or so. Even in Gupta's case, before his death, the company had put him on a lighter schedule. They kept him on a loose leash and provided him with a counselor to maintain a work-life balance. The buzz of Sunil Gupta's moving letter has pushed for more. The attitude of "If you can't take the heat, just get out of the kitchen," has declined significantly. Many banks currently give Saturdays off to junior bankers. Others offer one "protected weekend" each month for younger employees or ensure that juniors take four weekend days off each month. Yet still deaths are happening due to excessive distress, anxiety, depression, and collapse of well-being due to work overload and lack of sleep.

In Gupta's case, despite the "alleged" reduced schedule and life balance counselling, he was soon back to all-nighters, not going home for days at a stretch to satisfy his "annoyed" vice president and his father's ambitions for him. Similar cases have been reported at Zurich Insurance Group, Deutsche Bank, Russell Investments, and others, as published in a *Fortune* magazine story on this epidemic of finance market deaths (Better labelled now as "endemic"[17]). Sadly, this does not only ruin the lives of younger entrepreneurs longing for success and wealth under pressure from their bosses, but also top-ranking people and those who are already settled financially and socially. Ryan Crane, a JP Morgan executive director, for example, was found dead in such circumstances one day in 2014.

A similar incident occurred in 2018. Kate Spade, an American fashion designer and the founder of the designer brand Kate Spade New York was found deceased by her housekeeper in her Manhattan apartment in June 2018. Her death was ruled a suicide by hanging. The day after his wife's death, Andy Spade released a statement: "Kate suffered from depression and anxiety for many years". In the same month, Anthony Bourdain, an American celebrity chef, book author, and journalist who starred in programs focusing on the exploration of international culture and cuisine and won 15 renown awards, was found dead by suicide in his hotel room.

According to a study by Dr Michael Freeman, a clinical professor at the University of California, San Francisco, 30% of all entrepreneurs experience depression. This is really huge. We all have our stresses and anxieties. If the levels are minimal, they boost our energy and actions for progress. A bit more can be tolerated by our adaptation mechanisms, for which we have different capacities. Once the boundaries of our adaptations are crossed, though, our normal functioning abilities are disrupted, leading to lack of sleep,

---

17 A disease or a condition regularly found among particular people or in a certain area, as compared to an epidemic, which is a rapid spread of disease to a large number of people within a short period of time.

deterioration of work performance, disturbed social relations, sickness, loss of interest and joy, and abnormal eating habits. In the long term, depression becomes an issue that threatens life.

Entrepreneurs and other professionals who suffer from such issues feel entrapped. They get the sense that they are stuck in a cage that is getting smaller and smaller, with no way out. Collapsing or getting rid of their life are the only options "they can see". They can't imagine that they are able to make life-changing decisions out of all of this catastrophic existence. This is the moment they need urgent help before their dead bodies are found, whether in a deserted parking lot, in a busy street, or in their own home.

References: 23-35

Depression and Dreamland

- Doctors may be reluctant to diagnose depression with the absence of complaints about sleep.

- Poor sleep triggers depression and depression causes sleep issues. it is challenging to know which came first, sleep issues or depression.

- Insomnia occurs in 75% of patients with depression. 20% have obstructive sleep apnea (partial obstruction of the airway leading to reduced breathing) and 15% have hypersomnia (excessive daytime sleepiness).

- Insomnia increases your likelihood of depression 10 times.

- There is a trend to treat depression with limited sleep deprivation for short periods, but the resultant mood improvement is not long lasting.

- People with depression have more frequent dreams during night sleep. They also wake up frequently during the night. Thus, they tend to remember their dreams more. The impact of this tendency is variable according to the nature and content of these dreams. They may help in recovery or cause deterioration.

- A 2002 study from Rush-Presbyterian-St. Luke's Medical Center in Chicago conducted extensive dream analysis of 12 recently divorced women with signs of depression. The research continued over an eight-month period. The researchers found that, when dreams of the ex-spouse are seen in a distant manner, the divorced woman begins to recover and cope with this life change. Those who are not coping well have few dreams, and if the ex-partner appears in the dreams, they are seen in a negative role, often as weak, rejecting, or punishing.

References: 36-40.

6

THE NEW SIESTA

"Mr. Benn, Mr. Benn! Please wake up."

"Mr. Benn, the judge is talking to you."

"Mr. Benn. Please!"

The bailiff desperately tried to nudge the lawyer's chair, but as usual, the 72-year old was fully immersed in his dreamland.

"This is not going to work; it is useless. Leave him where he lives," interrupted Judge Lynn Hughes, before turning to the inmate. "George McFarland. I am asking you one more time. Are you still insisting that Mr. John Benn should continue to represent you for this trial?"

"Yes, sir. I am insisting that Mr. Benn is my sole lawyer."

Hughes asked the second question in the same sequence, as had repeatedly occurred over the previous few weeks.

"And are you still rejecting Mr. Sanford Melamed to co-counsel you?"

"Yes, sir. I am rejecting any one to represent me other than Mr. Benn."

Moments of courtroom silence—apart from Mr. John Benn's snoring—followed, before the case was adjourned once more.

The delay went on and on, but it did not overturn the sentence of capital punishment at the end. George McFarland was convicted of killing and robbery of a local grocer in 1992. He appealed against the court ruling, as his lawyer had frequently snoozed during the trial. Yet, his appeal was refuted as a second lawyer had been appointed for him. The appeal found that: "No one disputes that the lawyer's sleeping was pronounced, obvious, and frequent. But McFarland was never completely without counsel because a concerned judge had appointed another lawyer as co-counsel."

George McFarland

McFarland's rejection of Sanford Melamed, the second lawyer, and Benn's refusal to co-operate with him did not help the convict: "The court does not approve of a sleeping lawyer," Judge Hughes wrote. "This is unacceptable by an attorney in any case, and particularly in a case of this magnitude. The question before the court is whether the court of criminal appeals unreasonably applied federal constitutional law. It did not. McFarland was never completely without counsel."

This case in the Texas District Court is not unique. On many occasions, judges have been caught napping during legal proceedings.

The death sentence of alleged murderer Frederick Paine was over-turned after Judge Bill Beko of the Nevada Supreme Court nodded off during the trial.

At the Gloucester Crown Court, the trial of a man accused of rape was called off—at a cost of £35,000—when the defense counsel claimed that Judge Gabriel Hutton had been dozing during the hearing.

It is dreadful indeed to read these real-life stories of life or death decisions being made by people who were unconscious during pivotal proceedings before dispensing justice. But is this limited to court professions?

You definitely know the answer. Certainly not!

In a testimony before a Congressional Subcommittee on Health and the Environment, a Stanford University professor made this startling claim:

"The grounding of the Exxon Valdez, the near meltdown at Three Mile Island, the Bhopal catastrophe, and the explosion of the space shuttle Challenger [were] all caused totally or in part by sleepy people."

Well-documented incidents include, for example:

- Aeroflot Flight 3352 crashed in October 1984 into maintenance vehicles on the runway while landing in Omsk, Russia. The ground controller had been awake all night due to paternity commitments to his newborn twins. He fell asleep at work after allowing the workers to dry the runway following heavy rain. 178 people were killed in the accident. The controller later killed himself in prison.

- In March 2011, a tour bus driver crashed while returning from Connecticut to New York, causing many fatalities and injuries. Although the driver denied sleeping, an eye witness survivor reported that he was speeding and sleeping.

- A phone survey in 2010 concluded that 40% of U.S. drivers have "fallen asleep or nodded off" while driving. Most had been driving for less than an hour before they dozed off.

- The American Automobile Association estimates that one out of every six deadly car crashes are directly caused by drowsy driving.

- Kevin Roper, the Walmart truck driver who slammed into a limo bus carrying the comedian Tracy Morgan in 2014, had allegedly not slept for 24 hours before the accident.

TIME reported that a 2012 CDC National Health Survey found that on average, workers in the following occupations get the least amount of sleep:

- Home Health Aides
- Lawyers
- Police Officers
- Physicians, Paramedics
- Economists
- Social Workers
- Computer Programmers
- Financial Analysts
- Plant Operators
- Secretaries

A 2016 analysis conducted by the Rand Corporation measures the impact of sleep-deprived workers on the US economy to be $411bn a year, including lost productivity.

A Gallup poll reported that 51% of a random sample of adults admit that sleep deprivation, which causes both fatigue and drowsiness, negatively affects their job performance. An internet survey of 1,000 respondents conducted by Bill and Camille Anthony reported that 70% of them sometimes nap at work.

Photo by Karl-Erik Bennion

The vast majority of the instances mentioned above are collectively due to a type on nap called **"Recovery Nap"**; a nap that compensates for sleep loss when one is feeling tired after being up late or having interrupted sleep.

Other types of naps include:

Prophylactic Nap: Taken pre-emptively to prepare for sleep loss; when, for example, a night shift worker schedules naps before and during her shift to stay alert while working.

Appetitive Nap: For the joy of napping itself! It can be relaxing, help improve your mood and boost energy potential upon waking.

Essential Nap: During periods of sickness, you have a greater requirement for sleep. This is first due to the body's catabolic[18] state and second because your immune system triggers a response to fight infection and promote healing.

Fulfillment Nap: This is unique for children, especially infants, as they need more hours of sleeping, bearing in consideration that the growth hormone is more abundant during sleep. Fulfillment naps are regular in infants and toddlers, but they also occur spontaneously in children of all ages:

Infants (Up to One Year Old): May take one to four naps per day, lasting between 30 minutes and two hours.

Toddlers (One-Two Years Old): A study found that toddlers who napped could self-regulate their behavior and emotions more than toddlers who didn't.

Children (Over Two Years Old): Napping becomes less necessary.

Apart from the appetitive type, all other types are somewhat unintentional naps. However, voluntary intentional naps (like appetitive naps) have been common throughout history, especially in warmer

---

18 Catabolism is the set of metabolic pathways that breaks down molecules into smaller units that are oxidized to release energy or provide supply of more utilizable proteins.

countries such as in the south of Europe, the Middle East, Africa, Asia, and other places where the weather is too hot to carry on work at noon and during the early afternoon. The Spanish Siesta is one of the most renowned lunch breaks. Yet, it has mostly been abandoned now by the majority of Spaniards; it is too long (three hours) to align with the rhythms of modern life and working hours.

Modern science currently supports the **"power nap"**, a term coined by Cornell University social psychologist, Professor James Maas. It is a voluntary intentional nap during the working hours, encouraged to revitalize and restore alertness, performance, and learning ability. It also reverses the hormonal impact of a night of poor sleep, i.e. the damage of sleep deprivation. Consequently, by using this technique, we can avoid "unintentional involuntary" naps, which damage our health, impair our performance, endanger lives, and impose economic losses.

However, it has to be done the right way to work effectively, safely, and with maximum benefit.

A study from the University of Düsseldorf has proven superior memory recall after six minutes of sleep, suggesting that the onset of sleep stimulates memory processes of consolidation that remain effective even after waking up.

Another study from Flinders University is particularly significant for people with sleep deprivation. Individuals included in the research were restricted to five hours of sleep per night, then allowed to nap for variable periods during the day (lengths of 0 min, 5 min, 10 min, 20 min, and 30 minutes). The most powerful length was the 10-minute duration. It produced marked improvements in all outcome measures: sleep latency, sleepiness, fatigue, vigor, and cognitive performance. The surge of enhancements continued for more than 2.5 hours afterwards. The 5-minute nap was of less benefit. the 20-minute nap was also associated with benefits, but their emergence was delayed and did not continue for more than two hours. The 30-minute nap meant entry into deep sleep before being woken, which lead to a period of impaired alertness and below par performance immediately afterwards, indicating sleep inertia. However, the improvements started straightaway after that and lasted also for more than 2.5 hours.

The National Institute of Mental Health funded a team of doctors who wrote as a conclusion for their study published nearly two decades ago: "The bottom line is: we should stop feeling guilty about taking that 'power nap' at work."

Two British investigators, Horne and Reyner, tested the impact of cold air, radio, a break with no nap, a nap, caffeine pill vs. placebo, and a short nap preceded by caffeine on mildly sleep-deprived drivers in simulator experiments. A nap with caffeine was by far the most powerful in reducing accidents and subjective sleepiness as it assisted the body to get rid of the sleep-inducing chemical compound adenosine. It is described as a "double energy shot". Caffeine takes 20-30 minutes to induce alertness. So, the concept is to kick off at the exact time you wake up after the short nap with rejuvenation of your physical and mental resources (Stimulant nap).

Countries and cultures have different stands on napping at work.

A directive from the USA General Services Administration in November 2019 ordered: "All persons are prohibited from sleeping in federal buildings, except when such activity is expressly authorized by an agency official."

It was not clear what prompted the official directive cracking down on workers' napping. But in Japan, the stance is the opposite; they embrace the practice of Inemuri (sleeping wherever, whenever), daydreaming, or sleeping. It is not adopted only for workers' comfort or to boost their performance. It actually emerges from completely opposite roots of understanding. While the napping worker is regarded In the USA and similar cultures as a lazy person wasting the time and the money of the organization, in Japan, napping is regarded as a sign of overworking and devotion to the extent of exhaustion. Some Japanese businessmen even visit sleeping pods during the day to get some quiet, quality sleep time.

Nevertheless, the American culture started to change significantly on this matter a decade ago, at least in private organizations. It started at the Huffington Post, followed by Ben & Jerry's, Zappos, Nike, and others. All of them have now dedicated nap rooms.

Work Naps and Dreamland

- How should you nap the right way?

- Take It Early: Somewhere between 1 PM and 3 PM, so it doesn't interfere with your ability to fall asleep at bedtime.

- Make it a habit: Napping at the same time each day will make it easier for you to fall asleep quicker.

- Kick it up with coffee: Drinking coffee right before a short nap is scientifically proven to trigger the best performance as you wake up (a Stimulant nap).

- Optimum duration: 10-20 minutes can boost your job performance by as much as 34%. Five minutes is too short to make a difference, while 30 minutes will take you to a deep sleep and a cranky wake up.

- The Right Location: Find a quiet and private place. If that's not available, try your office, in your car, or on an outdoor bench.

- A prop: Slip on comfy socks, listen to a relaxing soundtrack, wipe lavender oil on your pulse points, or use a colorful blanket, a small pillow and an eye mask—anything you associate with your sleep ritual to help you nap faster. Sleep apps may also help.

References: 27, 41-48.

7

SUPERMAN OR A HYPOCRITIC SLEEPER: THOMAS EDISON

We owe Thomas Edison a lot when it comes to our vivid nights: our lit homes and streets, the hospital lights operating 24/7, our evening reading and study, the vehicles roaming through the darkness of the night, transporting people to their essential destinations, the longer productivity of work after sunset, and all the innumerable merits of electric lamps. On the contrary, Edison owes us the couple of hours that the artificial light has subtracted from the average sleep of the contemporary human being. We may pardon him for that, although Michael Jackson, Sarvshreshth Gupta, the likes of Samar and Lisa Bernard, and other people whose lives have crumbled due to sleep deprivation would probably disagree.

The anti-sleep ideology Edison propagated since the end of the 19th century is deplorable. Human civilization undeniably needed and was enormously advanced by Edison's artificial lamp, in addition to his other 1,092 inventions. However, Edison's scorns of the value of sleep for human wellbeing was extreme to the point of fanaticism. As the genius was—and still is—regarded as the most splendid icon of achievement in modern age, his ideology of discarding rest for the sake of productivity has spread like wildfire within the elite of various life fields. From Charles Lindbergh[19] to Winston Churchill,

---

19 An American aviator, military officer, author, inventor, and activist. At the age of 25 in 1927, he gained world fame for making a nonstop flight from New York City to Paris in a sleepless 33.5 hours. He admitted having hallucinations closer to the end of his journey.

then Sam Walton[20], Margaret Thatcher, Bill Clinton, Jack Dorsey[21], and Donald Trump, it has consistently been claimed that working for longer extended hours at the expense of rest is heroic and a definite sign of accomplishment, super aptitude, and deserved leadership.

In his book, *Dangerously Sleepy: Overworked Americans and the Cult of Manly Wakefulness,* Alan Derickson[22] wrote, "Edison spent considerable amounts of his own and his staff's energy on publicizing the idea that success depended in no small part in staying awake to stay ahead of the technological and economic competition." According to the author, nobody "did more to frame the issue as a simple choice between productive work and unproductive rest."

The Edisonian lifestyle was widely promoted by media at the dawn of the 20th century, especially in children's books and magazines: "One juvenile motivational text featured a photo of Edison with a group of workers identified as his Insomnia Squad," Derickson highlighted.

Edison worked for up to 100 hours per week and forced his employees onto the same schedule.

"At first the boys had some difficulty in keeping awake, and would go to sleep under stairways and in corners. We employed watchers to bring them out, and in time they got used to it," Edison said in an 1889 interview with *Scientific American.*

In his book, *Thomas A. Edison: The Man, His Work and His Mind* published at the peak time of Edison's success in 1913, John Hubert Greusel wrote about Edison's staff: "When they fell from sheer exhaustion, he seemed to begrudge the brief hours they were sleeping."

---

20 An American businessman and entrepreneur best known for founding the retailers Walmart and Sam's Club.

21 Founder of both Square and Twitter.

22 Author and professor of Labor Studies and History at Pennsylvania State University.

Edison was quoted more than once: "There is really no reason why men should go to bed at all." "a waste of time, heritage from our cave days."

In *Sleep Thieves,* published in 1996, professor of Psychology Stanley Coren quoted Edison: "When I went through Switzerland in a motor-car, so that I could visit little towns and villages, I noted the effect of artificial light on the inhabitants. Where water power and electric light had been developed, everyone seemed normally intelligent. Where these appliances did not exist, and the natives went to bed with the chickens, staying there until daylight, they were far less intelligent."

The fanatism of the inventions' mastermind (not really so otherwise) never stopped: "For myself I never found need of more than four– or five-hours' sleep in the twenty-four. I never dream. It's real sleep. When by chance I have taken more I wake dull and indolent. We are always hearing people talk about 'loss of sleep' as a calamity. They better call it loss of time, vitality and opportunities. Just to satisfy my curiosity I have gone through files of the British Medical Journal and could not find a single case reported of anybody being hurt by loss of sleep." Of course, this was a 100% false claim even by the standards of the medical knowledge available 100 years ago. Yet, no scientists publicly challenged this concept and its propaganda carried on.

And it was sheer hypocrisy. Indubitable evidence proves that Edison had cots in all of his work places. He was sleeping multiple times during the day, everywhere: in his office, in his lab, in his library, in the fields, in public areas (in addition to his 4-5 hours night sleep).

Actually, no famous scientist was pictured sleeping more than Edison:

TEARING OFF A NAP AFTER 72 HOURS
OF CONTINUOUS WORK.   OCT. 1912.

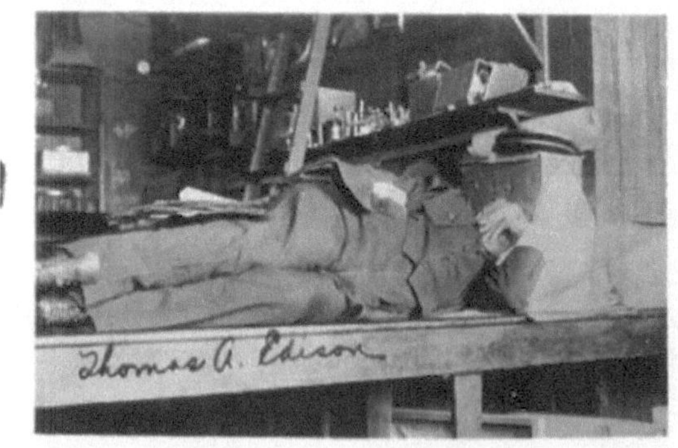
Thomas A. Edison

One account of the setup in West Orange laboratory was written by Frank Lewis Dyer and Thomas Martin in *Edison: His Life and Inventions* (public library):

"As one is about to pass out of the library attention is arrested by an incongruity in the form of a cot, which stands in an alcove near the door. Here Edison, throwing himself down, sometimes seeks a short rest during especially long working hours. Sleep is practically instantaneous and profound, and he awakes in immediate and full possession of his faculties, arising from the cot and going directly "back to the job" without a moment's hesitation…"

There are even more revelations admitted by Edison himself in his diary of the July 12, 1885, which was published in 1971:

"Awakened at 5:15 AM My eyes were embarrassed by the sunbeams. Turned my back to them and tried to take another dip into oblivion. Succeeded. Awakened at 7 AM Thought of Mina, Daisy, and Mamma G. Put all three in my mental kaleidoscope to obtain a new combination a la Galton. Took Mina as a basis, tried to improve her beauty by discarding and adding certain features borrowed from Daisy and Mamma G. A sort of Raphaelized beauty, got into it too deep, mind flew away and I went to sleep again. Awakened at 8:15 AM. … Arose at 9 o'clock, came down stairs expecting it was too late for breakfast. It wasn't."

On July 14, in contradiction of his claim that he never dreams, Edison noted:

"In evening went out on sea wall. Noticed a strange phosphorescent light in the west, probably caused by a baby moon just going down Chinaward, thought at first the Aurora Borealis had moved out west. Went to bed early dreamed of a demon with eyes four hundred feet apart."

And on July 19:

"Slept as sound as a bug in a barrel of morphine."

On one occasion, Edison was disappointed that his invention of a printing machine did not work. So, he kept on working nonstop for 60 hours, until he overcame the fault, then slept continuously for 30 hours.

***

Thomas Edison was not superhuman. Like all of us, he needed to sleep and dream. He was sleep-deprived on a regular basis due to his "super" hunger for learning, inventing, and achieving. He made up for his sleep deprivation with repeated naps during the day; what is known in modern sleep science as recovery naps. They rejuvenate the mental fitness and the physical stamina; hence their other name is "power naps".

Edison had a breathtaking passion and joy of science and invention. He did not seem to enjoy spending time on anything else. To enforce devotion to work for all people in the same way is neither fair, natural, nor applicable. Most of us like to relax, enjoy hobbies, have a social and family life, read beyond our work references, and cherish entertainment; in short, life-work balance.

For some reason, which was possibly genuine—such as enhancement of work productivity—the virtuoso inventor dishonestly and widely spread the concept of sleep unnecessity, giving counterfeit examples from his own life to bolster his claims. The vast majority of famous people creating this kind of non-stop work, non-sleep propaganda about themselves to enhance their leadership capability are doing exactly the same. If they are not, they should be treated like sleep-deprived pilots and drivers: banned from the steering wheel. What Edison enhanced as a progressive notion 100 years ago is now scientifically regarded as backward thinking.

References: 49-52.

Dreamland Deprivation Hazards

- Deterioration of short and long-term memory (33% increase in dementia risk).

- Lack of concentration, problem solving skills, and creativity (3-5 years brain aging).

- Escalation of anxiety and depression.

- Higher accident and injury proneness (6,000 fatal car crashes/year in the USA).

- Weaker immune system (Risk of catching viral infections multiplied by 3).

- Increased risk of high blood pressure and heart disease (by 48%).

- Increased risk of diabetes (multiplied by 3).

- Predisposition to obesity (50% higher risk).

- Lower sex drive.

- Quicker skin aging.

- Hallucinations.

- Augmented risk of cancer (36% for colorectal cancer).

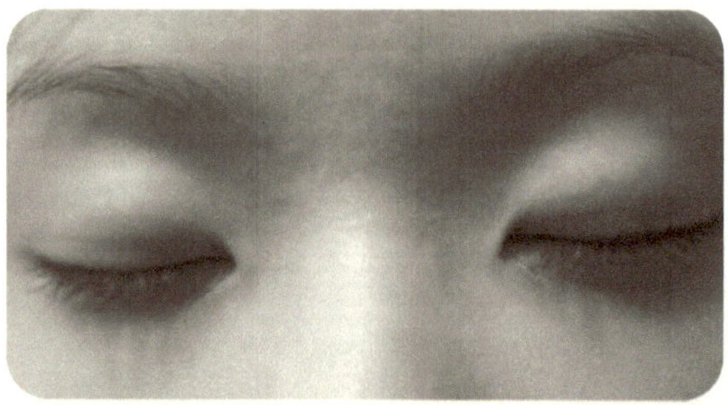

References: 53-58.

NOBODY WOULD
TELL SAMAR

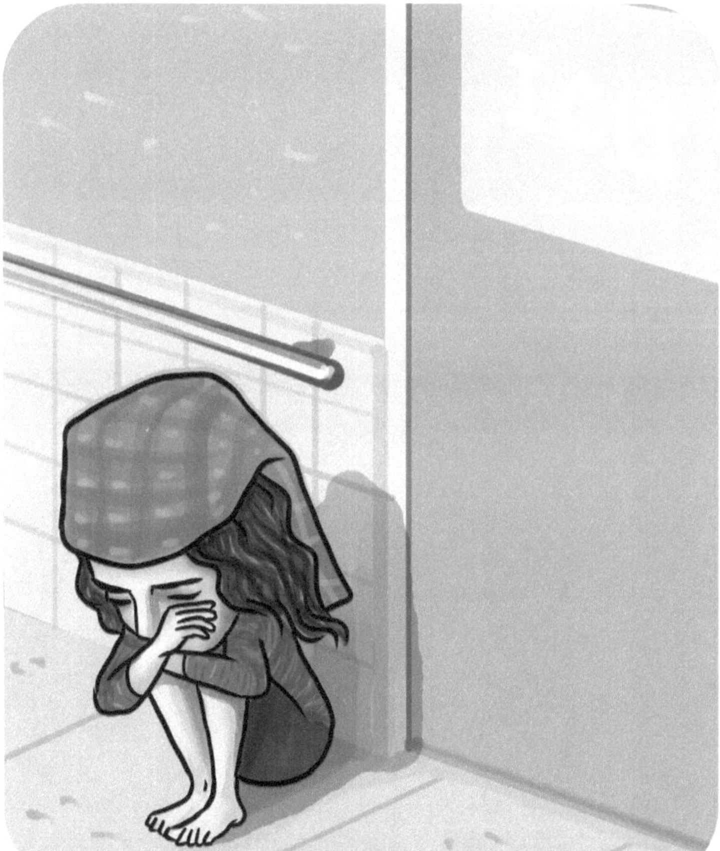

She has been squatting on the floor next to the critical care unit for three hours so far, and all efforts to move her have been in vain. They have tried all possible ways apart from violence. Even the hospital manager tried. Their refraining from calling the security guard to remove her by force is merely out of consideration for her current state of mind and emotions. Feelings of guilt must be shattering her now.

24 hours earlier:

04:30: Samar woke up, but this is a metaphor, as she has barely slept in the first place. Time to prepare breakfast and school meals for Mohammed and Shereen.

05:30: Carrying Mostafa to Shaimaa. The toddler has to stay at the neighbors' until she returns from work. Baby-sitting is unaffordable in this part of Cairo. So, it is done in return of favors.

05:45: Running to catch the microbus[23]. If missed, who knows when the next one is. Madame Inas is very fussy about punctuality.

06:20: A short nap on the microbus was interrupted by a fare squabble. The driver insists on 6.50[24] (40 cents) but the passenger would

---

23 Microbuses are small buses, the cheapest widely available means of transport in many countries, especially in poorer areas.

24 In Egyptian pounds: As per 2020 currency conversion rates, 16 Egyptian pounds approximately = 1 USD.

pay only a fiver (30 cents). "OK. Everybody off! I'm not moving until he pays." The driver switched the engine off.

Samar looked around. It is literally the middle of nowhere. She'll pay then to resolve the dispute. She can't afford Madame Inas' wage deductions. The driver's trick has worked again.

07:07: Out of breath, Samar is at the door of Madame Inas' villa. She had to dash through the luxurious compound, a desperate shot to arrive on time; nearly made it. Probably the lady will accept a seven-minute delay. She needs the services of her house maid as well.

"The carpets need to be dusted; all 11 carpets. Curtains as well; all of them. But you can start with car washing as usual. Don't worry about the garden today. Gamal is here today to look after it. You can clean the swimming pool instead. We emptied the water last night. By the way, I didn't like your job with the chandeliers last time. You have to do them again, I'm afraid, and be careful with the vases. Break one and lose your wage for the rest of the year.

I'll call the supermarket after breakfast. I just prepared the list of cooking for the next three days. Perhaps you can start after you do the washing and the ironing. Pay special attention to the toilets. The boys made a mess after their football. And don't forget, whole house wiping, not only vacuum cleaning. You already know about the coronavirus and stuff…"

As Inas continued, Samar had already rolled her sleeves and trousers up. She knows the lady won't shut up soon.

13:30: In the corner of the kitchen, curled in on herself, weeping in silence. The silence was hurting more than the weeping. 27 years had passed since she left her village. Her father was a "donkey merchant", as he called himself, a two-word description with one lie; he did not have any donkeys to merchandize. He forced her out of school as he did with her older sisters to engage them as house maids in the big city, the capital. He would confiscate all of their earnings: "What do you need the money for? You are eating and drinking where you work." This is how he responded whenever the girls asked for even a share. Actually, he was selling his daughters not donkeys.

Married 14 years ago, her husband was not any better. He was reluctant to work, instead sitting at the café all day long, relying on her income. He was supposed to be a grocer, but spent some time in jail after stealing from the shop. Afterwards, nobody wanted to employ him. Last year, he dumped her for the hairdresser a couple of blocks away.

"What's wrong with you? Why are you crying?" asked Inas.

"Nothing. I'm all right. I finished all what you asked me to do. Can I leave now? I need to go as the kids will return from school soon."

"You can go. Listen. Take these. They will help you get through life's adversities." Inas handed over to her a canister of small pills, her left over anti-depressants.

20:40: Samar is on her way back for the second time to the small basement room where she lives with her three children. Earlier, she returned to prepare their dinner, but had to leave for her second job in another house at 16:30. Otherwise, she wouldn't be able to make ends meet; poor ends but even still, extremely tough to meet.

21:35: Heavy traffic; the 45 minutes journey home is now extended for more than 90 minutes, deducted from her presumed sleep time.

00: 05: Can't sleep. The wedding on the roof of the building is now at its climax. The songs broadcasted to the whole neighborhood are deafening. Samar got off the bed, stood up and walked to her small kitchen in a sleep deprivation wobble. Slowly and inaudibly, Mostafa followed her. It seems that the noise has interrupted the youngster's slumber as well. Samar's sight fell on the canister she took from Inas in the afternoon. She grabbed it, sat on the chair, and dozed off.

04:35: She has been squatting on the floor next to the critical care unit for three hours so far, and all efforts to move her have been in vain. They have tried all possible ways apart from violence. Even the hospital manager tried. Their refraining from calling the security guard to remove her by force is merely out of consideration for her current state of mind and emotions. Feelings of guilt must be shattering her now.

Mostafa's life is on the brink. The doctors have emptied his stomach, but they are not sure how much of the anti-depressant medicine has leaked into his systems. The number of tablets he ingested should be fatal. Time, monitoring, and further tests will give a verdict within the next few hours.

At the moment, Samar has been up for more than 24 hours, but is more attentive than she has ever been. She shouldn't have snoozed with that canister accessible. She views herself as having killing her own beloved child by neglect, and that is indeed the prejudice of all these people passing by her here and now. She feels their gazes stabbing her veraciously. And she is right. If the poor soul passes away tonight, tomorrow all media outlets, Facebook and Twitter posts, TV programs, her neighborhood, employers, the prosecution authorities, the social services, and a whole country will be convicting her as a negligent parent, unworthy of motherhood.

Nobody will tell Samar that she is the first-hand victim:

The victim of inhumane sleep deprivation for the sake of providing her own children with life essentials, so a description of "negligent" does not fit.

The victim of a miserable everyday life, enforced upon her by the reckless, self-centered men meant to be caring for her.

The victim of lack of a welfare system to support the weakest links in the community.

The victim of incompetence of laws and regulations governing interests of 21st-century citizens.

The victim of inequality in its severest form, eroding the human wealth of nations.

The victim of a neoliberal ideology, that has ruled the world over the past 40 years; an era where billions of women and children like Samar and Mostafa have been left behind by the state to be torn apart by the canines of social injustice monsters.

Social Injustice and Dreamland

- The income of 33% of Egyptian families is totally provided by women. This is extremely tough considering that they are full-time wives and mothers as well.

- 26% of these women live below the poverty threshold (2 USD/day).

- 25% of Egyptian women are illiterate, being forced out of schools early in primary education.

- Worldwide, almost half of humanity live on less than $5.50 a day.

- The 22 richest men of the world have more wealth than all the women of Africa.

- The unpaid care work done by women is 10.8 trillion USD a year, three times the entire global tech industry.

References: 27, 59-63.

CONFESSIONS OF NIGHT SHIFT DOCTORS

In 2017, the ACGME (Accreditation Council for Graduate Medical Education) in the USA decided to increase work hours to 28-hour shifts for new doctors.

In response to this change, KevinMD, a popular physician's social media outlet, published these anonymous confessions (de-identified with some patient details changed to protect confidentiality):

"I did my internship in internal medicine and residency in neurology before laws existed to regulate resident hours. My first two years were extremely brutal, working 110 to 120 hours/week, and up to 40 hours straight. I got to witness colleagues collapse unconscious in the hallway during rounds, and I recall once falling asleep in the bed of an elderly comatose woman while trying to start an IV[25] on her in the wee hours of the morning."

"I ran a red light driving home in residency after a 36-hour shift. Got pulled over. It was sobering: I was not fit to use my driver's license, but I had just been using my MEDICAL license for over a day non-stop!"

"I have made numerous medication errors from being over tired. I also more recently misread an EKG[26] because I was so tired, I literally couldn't see straight. She actually had a subarachnoid hemorrhage,

---

25 Intravenous: Access to veins for administering fluids and medications or withdrawing blood samples.

26 Electrocardiograph: Measuring the electrical activity of the heart.

and by misreading the EKG, I spent too much time on her heart and didn't whisk her back to CT[27] when she came in code blue[28]. She died."

"After a 36-hour shift, I fell asleep and began dreaming while walking home—repeatedly. It was a four-block walk."

"I fell asleep multiple times at the light at the intersection right at my neighborhood after call. I would see home was close and relax just enough. I had a baby, and I was so afraid of forgetting him in the back seat. If I ever had him with me, I would put his bag in the front with me and my stuff in the back with him. Luckily, nothing bad happened in either situation, but I just got lucky."

"As a resident in a surgical specialty, my program routinely violated work hours, yet our attending physicians kept talking about how lucky we are because we have "work hour restrictions." To fool my brain into not stopping, I'd lie to myself. I'd tell myself that if I just got out of bed at 3:30 one more time I could go to bed early that night, or if I just got through a few more notes, I could go home and finish the rest tomorrow. I thought I could just keep going at that pace and nothing terrible would happen until I woke up in the ICU[29] and a doctor told me I had tried to kill myself."

"In general surgery residency, I had one week in which I worked 125 hours ... I did a weekend of 72 hours in which I only got four hours of sleep. I would secretly hope to get in a car accident and maybe break a leg so that I would be forced to take off from work ... just so I could get some rest."

---

27 Computed tomography: A scan which combines a series of X-ray images taken from different angles and uses computer processing to create cross-sectional images of tissues and provide detailed information.

28 Hospitals often use code names to alert their staff to an emergency or other event. Code blue indicates a cardiac or respiratory arrest.

29 Intensive care unit.

"During intern year at a program with a nominal 80-hour work week, I worked 100 hours per week for most of a month. I was interviewing a patient when I suddenly realized that I could not remember what I had just asked. I excused myself abruptly and rushed down the hall where I collapsed on the bathroom floor. I leaned against the wall and felt relaxed for the first time in weeks. My face was wet, and I realized I was sobbing. I was so unaware of how exhausted and impaired I had become. I cried because I was tired, and also because the patient I was seeing deserved better attention and care than I was capable of providing. I couldn't remember any details of his chest pain or risk factors for heart attack. I couldn't even remember his name or his face. Only that he was friendly and he trusted me. I felt intensely guilty for not being able to stay awake, let alone think like a doctor. I nodded off while crying, propped up against the wall. I woke up and forgave myself. I think I was away from him for less than 10 minutes. I walked back into his exam room and said, "Where were we? Let's start at the beginning to make sure I get this right. Because what you are saying is really important." That month during my evaluation, my program director told me that my total number of work hours was a sign of inefficiency. I later learned that others were also working 80 to 100 hours per week, but they falsified their hours to avoid criticism."

"I have fallen asleep at the wheel thousands of times since medical school. I literally would wake up the next day in my work clothes and not even remember leaving the hospital. I drive from 45 min to four hours to rural hospitals now and in training, currently working up to seven straight 24s in a row."

"I was post-call after a 30-hour shift and rear-ended a car while driving uphill. No one was hurt, but I remember the guy saying, 'you hit me driving uphill.'"

"I was so sleep deprived that I'd fall asleep while writing patient notes and write my dreams into the notes. I've fallen asleep on a pile of charts only to have the nurses cover me with blankets. I woke panicked because I was hours behind in my work. I've fallen asleep standing up in surgery and witnessed my attending doctors fall asleep while doing surgery. I actually passed out at the end of a 36-hour shift and woke up on a stretcher in the recovery room."

"A dear friend from med school died during her neurosurgery residency. Drove over a median into a tractor-trailer after a 30+ hour shift. She left behind her family, including a twin sister and her fiancé. She was 30."

"I had married the year before residency, and for that first two years, I was either at work or asleep, so didn't see my wife, and it was the start of the erosion of the relationship that led years later to divorce. I also suffered permanent health problems from extreme sleep deprivation. Prior to residency, I slept fine (8 hours per night) and had regular bowel habits. Since my internship, I developed life-long severe insomnia, and went for decades on four to five hours of sleep/night, as well as severe constipation, using the toilet about every five days."

"I was at one of the most humane programs in the country, yet as an intern I would frequently gag on water while trying to drink. I knew by then that stroke patients and others with neurologic impairment had swallowing problems. Mine always went away while working less than 50 hours per week."

"During internship, I was driving home after a 30-hour call. It was dark and rainy out. The usual road I took home was closed, so after some roundabout driving, I got on to the garden state parkway in NJ[30] going in the wrong direction. Thankfully a police car saw me and pulled me over as I realized I was going into oncoming traffic. He escorted me all the way home."

---

30 New Jersey, a state in the Mid-Atlantic region of the Northeastern United States.

"I was working in the NICU[31] and commuting 45 miles each way to and from the hospital when I was involved in a serious car accident in which my car was completely totaled. My program directors were upset that I did not make it back to work the next day (as I had to deal with insurance, get a rental car, etc.) Before this, I had a perfect driving record."

"I was struck down with a very severe depression in the context of emotional conflicts and severe sleep deprivation, after doing a surgical rotation with every other night call and lots of degrading comments from the surgeons recommending that I go into nursing or teaching instead since those were "good professions for women." This was 1983. I was supported in the sense that I missed six weeks of medical school without censure while I was too debilitated to move physically. I spent those weeks mainly sitting in a corner of my apartment, crying, and seeing my psychiatrist once/week for therapy and meds."

"I have gained easily a hundred pounds over the years in part from eating to stay awake. The state police have woken me up on the side of the road many times when I pulled off the highway to sleep because I couldn't stay awake until the next exit."

＊＊＊

A series of well-recognized studies at the beginning of the 21st century have proven that nurses who work longer than 13 hours shifts report:

---

31 Neonatal intensive care unit.

1. a 1.9- to 3.3-fold increased odds of making an error in patient care,

2. a significantly increased risk of suffering a needlestick injury, exposing them to an increased risk of acquiring hepatitis, HIV, or other bloodborne illnesses, and

3. significant decrease in vigilance on the job.

The Joint Commission Journal on Quality and Patient Safety published in 2007 a report on the "Effects of Health Care Provider Work Hours and Sleep Deprivation on Safety and Performance."

The report concluded that "extended-duration work shifts significantly increase fatigue and impair performance. Residents' traditional work shifts of 24–30 consecutive hours unquestionably increased the risk of serious medical errors and diagnostic mistakes. Likewise, long work hours increase the risk that nurses and doctors will suffer an occupational injury with potentially devastating long-term consequences and increase the risk of motor vehicle crashes, a leading cause of mortality among young adults. Thus, both from the standpoint of providers and patients, the hours routinely worked by health care providers in the United States are unsafe."

Residents' Motor Vehicle Crashes, Near-Miss Motor Vehicle Accidents, and Percutaneous Injuries Reported Relative to the Duration of Work Shifts

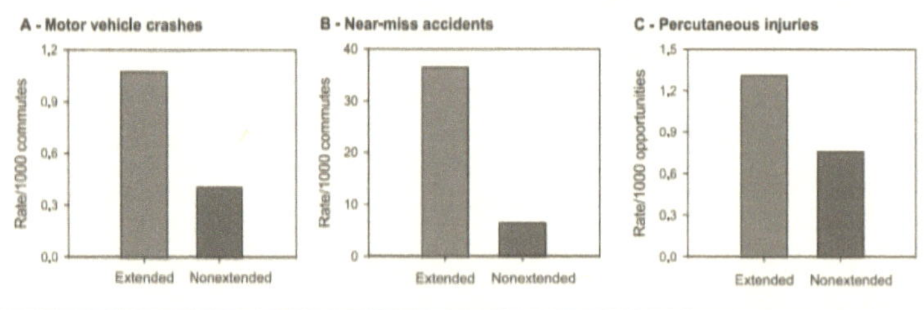

A 2014 study by researchers in Saudi Arabia advised that hospitals should have nap rooms for **staff**, especially doing night shifts for short naps rejuvenation and to minimize the chances of doctors and nurses' errors caused by tiredness, as well as post-shift traffic accidents.

In 2019, a report authored by Coren Thomas in *Daily Nurse* conveyed data from studies conducted by NASA and the U.S. military on cognitive function following prolonged hours of sustained wakefulness.

Here are some examples:

After 24 hours of uninterrupted wakefulness, the impairment is comparable to that of someone who has had two to three alcoholic drinks.

When you've been awake for 17 hours, your cognitive and psychomotor performance becomes roughly equal to that of someone who has consumed one to two alcoholic drinks.

Staying awake for 24 hours creates a condition comparable to having a blood alcohol level of roughly .10%, which is over the legal limit for driving.

*****

Night shifts are mostly done by junior nurses and doctors, whose voices are less prominent within the profession and the community. Hence, raising concerns on such a sensitive issue may be misunderstood as a cheap attempt to escape the call of duty. Therefore, in 2020, risky healthcare practices still abound, and these seem set to linger for an indefinite time into the future.

Night Shifts and Dreamland

- Night workers are unfairly affected, getting approximately two to four hours less sleep than normal.

- Our bodily rhythms are set by sunlight. Exposure to bright light when it's time to sleep makes it harder for the body to produce melatonin, a sleep hormone.

- Over time, sleep deprivation leads to an increased risk for heart disease, gastrointestinal problems, and reproductive issues, in addition to cancer.

- In one study, researchers had mice imitate the schedules of shift workers: The rodents' brain cells began dying off in few days, and the damage was permanent. Another study on 147 adult humans found that the sleep disadvantaged had actively shrinking brains.

- No amount of "catch up" sleep can ever reverse the effects of sleep loss on the body.

References: 64-71.

15 MINUTES ONLY. I'LL DO WHATEVER YOU WANT!

In October 2018, a video went viral on Egyptian social media. The video featured Mohammed, a six-year-old primary school student in his classroom, heavily weeping while begging his teacher to allow him sleep for just 15 minutes: "I'll do whatever you want, but let me sleep please, only for 15 minutes."

The teacher tried to calm him down: "You'll be home in a little while, love."

As the child was inconsolable, the school management called his father to pick him up earlier. Such occurrences are not unusual and have been so for decades in different parts of the world, but the video drew lots of attention, with subsequent noise both within the community and on social media. Some regarded it as funny, others blamed the official who recorded it and posted it on social media without parental permission, and many felt pity for the adorable kid. The parents formally complained before the incident got wiped away after few days by the next trends on social media. However, the vital questions the video raised have not been answered nor even discussed:

- How common is sleep deprivation in children?
- What are the reasons?
- How is it affecting their learning, quality of life, development, growth, and future?
- What are the solutions?

***

In fact, the sleep statistics for children are quite shocking:

- 54% of boys and 62% of girls are sleep deprived.

- 20% of parents are concerned about their children's sleep; most parents of children with lack of sleep are unaware that a problem exists in the first place.

- Every 30 minutes of extra sleep make a significant difference in school performance.

- The average child is sleeping 1.3 hours less than their requirements every night.

- The future of these little angels with sleep insufficiency is threatened by the following risks:

    - 91% overweight
    - 97% depression
    - 105% proneness to injury
    - 118% weaker immunity
    - 190% cognitive deterioration
    - 247% more behavioral issues/hour of sleep deficiency

But why are children sleeping so little nowadays?

In the era of screens, the answer is obvious: children stay up longer watching TV, using their mobile phones, iPads, video games consoles, and many other gadgets. More than 50% of teenagers in one study reported active engagement on cell phones after bedtime. It is not only about being busy with activities. Actually, the nature of these activities is pretty stressful, involving fight and flight responses, increasing the heart rate and blood pressure, in addition to stimulant brain activity.

Similar to adults who hurry to do everything in limited available hours, children (especially adolescents) also struggle to finish everything within their daily agendas: school, homework, playing, social media, watching, and sports training or practicing their hobbies. Some older children are even working in afterschool jobs.

Parents coming home late can also inflict a negative effect on their kids' sleeping habits, especially if they themselves do not go to bed until late. Some cultures have the habit of the whole community sleeping late, so retail, entertainment, and leisure carry on continuously or until the early hours of the next day.

Children eating high calories, high carbohydrate foods, and consuming high energy drinks find it difficult to sleep early.

Some children cannot help their sleep issues, as they have medical problems, whether physical or psychological, that cause sleep disruption. This requires specialist advice, support, and possibly medications. The most challenging matter here is the vicious cycle of sleep disruption and medical problems, as sleep disruption can lead to medical illnesses like obesity and behavioral disorders. Obesity causes regurgitation and obstructive sleep apnea[32], which in their turn interrupt sleep. Behavioral problems also make sleep disruption worse and the cycle continues. You do not know which problem started the cycle and which treatment cuts off the cycle.

How can parents know that their child is lacking sufficient sleep?

A child with mild sleep deprivation will find it difficult to wake up in the morning, yawn frequently during the day, want to consume stimulant drinks like sugary high energy beverages, and struggle to learn new information.

When the sleep insufficiency is more significant, the child may fall asleep again after being woken up and need repeated attempts of stimulation, complain of feeling tired, want to nap during the day, fall asleep or seem drowsy at school, and have increased stress and impulsivity throughout the day.

In severe sleep deprivation, the child prefers to lie down during the day, even if it means missing activities they like. The child will lose interest, motivation, and attention, be very forgetful, get blurred vision, and have excessive mood swings with irritability.

---

32 The most common sleep-related breathing disorder. It is characterized by recurrent episodes of complete or partial obstruction of the upper airway leading to reduced or absent breathing during sleep.

The way forward

To tackle the problem, the whole family need to be involved, particularly if cultural factors are contributing. Family dynamics play a vital role both in creating the difficulty and potentially in managing it.

Essential steps often include:

- Avoiding evening naps.

- Cutting down on foods and drinks with high caffeine and sugar content, especially late in the day.

- Reduction of afterschool activities.

- Refraining from using sleep as a punishment.

- A breeze of fresh air close to bedtime.

- Heading to the bedroom while the child is tired but still awake and avoidance of the habit of sleeping with the parents or shifting to own bed after falling asleep.

- A stuffed soft toy and a special blanket may help. This is called a "Transitional object".

- Fixing sleep and wake up times even on weekends and holidays, in addition to observation of a bedtime routine limited to relaxing habits like reading or listening to soothing music.

- Stopping high-energy activities two hours prior to bedtime with a curfew for screens.

- Using the bedroom for sleep only, not for play or study. Gadgets should not be used there.

- Keeping the bedroom cool, dark, and quiet. White noise is sometimes of benefit.

- Black out curtains or night lamp if the child is scared of darkness.

- Minimization of noise for the rest of the house.

What about a later start of school day?

A study published on December 12, 2018, in the journal *Science Advances*, found that delaying the start time of high schools in the USA by one hour boosts the duration of sleep students get daily by more than 30 minutes and improves academic performance (4.5% higher grades).

Another impressive study published one year earlier in *Frontiers in Human Neuroscience* was conducted on British schools. It concluded that 10 AM is the optimum time for the start of the school day, with even better performance and reduced illness to less than half.

Whether such change is realistic and logistically feasible is another question. Nonetheless, the concept is certainly worth at least a rational, open-minded, comprehensive discussion.

Dreamland Requirements by Age

- 0-3 months: 15-16 hours/day
- 4-11 months: 13-15 hours/day
- 1-2 years: 12-14 hours/day
- 3-5 years: 11-12 hours/day
- 6-12 years: 10 hours/day
- 13-17 years: 9 hours/day
- 18-64 years: 8 hours/day
- 65+ years: 7-8 hours/day

References: 72-80.

HIS EYES COULD NOT DANCE: MICHAEL JACKSON

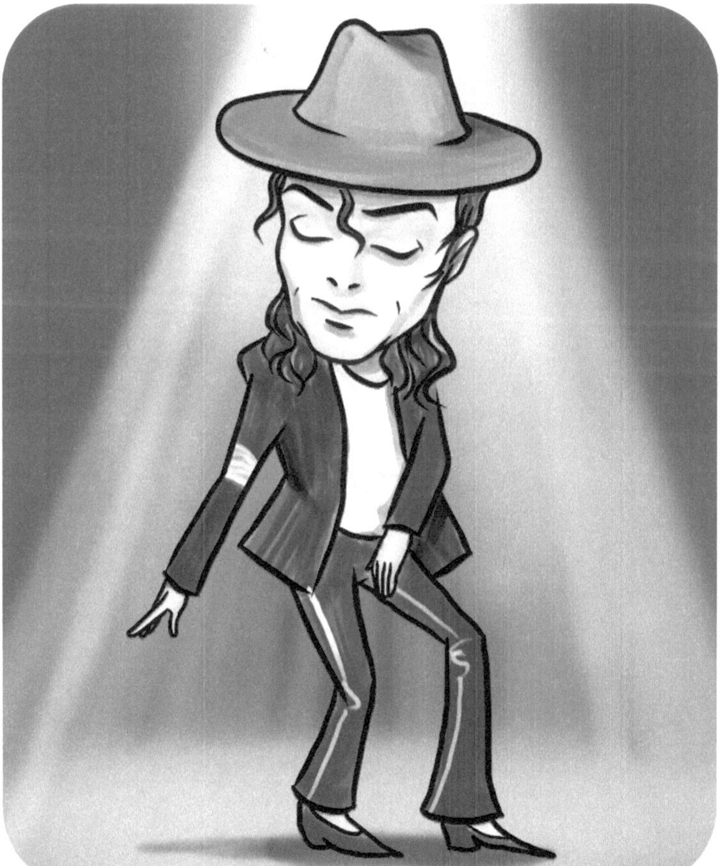

It is June 25, 2009, at 3 PM.

Google is under DDoS attack[33]. Or is it?

There are millions of simultaneous analogous searches.

Block these searches for 30 minutes please, until we clarify the situation.

But it is not only Google. Twitter has crashed as well.

And Wikipedia?

Yes. Nearly a million visitors within one hour to the same page.

There are reported outages on several popular websites.

AOL collapsed for 40 minutes.

It's to be expected; the whole world's internet traffic is 20% higher.

But it is not a cyber-attack. It is real news. Michael Jackson has just died at 2:26 PM.

---

33 In computing, a denial-of-service (DDoS) attack is a cyber-attack in which the perpetrator seeks to make a machine or network resource unavailable to its intended users by disrupting services of a host connected to the Internet.

***

3 months earlier: I want the milk

"I stopped drinking Red Bull Cherilyn; only your fresh organic juices, but still I cannot sleep all night," a frustrated Michael told his holistic healthcare nurse.

"You still don't feel well? You look much healthier to me. I believe that Myers cocktails[34] are helping you," Cherilyn Lee responded.

"I need something more. I won't be able to rehearse for *This Is It*[35]. "A sleep specialist maybe?" Cherilyn suggested.

Michael did not seem to be impressed.

She added, "At least cut down on the lights and music in your bedroom."

Disregarding Michael: "I'm thinking of the milk."

"What milk???!!"

---

34 Intravenous (IV) vitamin therapy. Medical experts warn that they do not have any benefits and may be harmful due to risk of infection and possible allergic reaction. The name is attributed to Baltimore physician John A. Myers. Naturopathic doctors in the United States and Canada often administer the IV drip in clinics and health spas.

35 A concert series scheduled to start on July 13, 2009, but cancelled due to Michael Jackson's death 18 days prior on June 25. On March 11, two days before pre-sale began, an extra 40 dates were added to meet high demand, bringing the number of shows to 50. More than 1.5 million fans caused two sites offering pre-sale tickets to crash within minutes of going online. In the space of four hours, 750,000 tickets were sold. Two million people tried to buy pre-sale tickets in the space of 18 hours.

Michael replied: "The milk I had 12 years ago to make me sleep. German doctors gave it to me in a drip. It was magic; the best sleep I ever had." "I'll get you its name."

He added, "Propofol was the name."

While Michael contacted AEG[36], the organizer of his concerts, to help with arrangements for Propofol infusions, Cherilyn researched the drug in her Physicians' Desk Reference manual: "Propofol is a medication that results in a decreased level of consciousness and a lack of memory for events. Its uses include the starting and maintenance of general anesthesia and procedural sedation.

Common side effects of propofol include an irregular heart rate, low blood pressure, and the cessation of breathing. Other serious side effects may include seizures, infections due to improper use and addiction. It has been referred to as milk of amnesia (a play on 'milk of magnesia'), because of the milk-like appearance of the intravenous preparation."

Cherilyn, "It's not something you want to use at home, Michael." She added, "It isn't a safe medication, not for insomnia. I understand you want to be 'knocked out'—but what if you don't wake up?"

"Cherilyn, I'll be ok. I've talked with doctors. I only need someone to monitor me with equipment while I sleep. You don't understand; doctors are telling me it's safe just as long as I am being monitored. If you want really to help me, please find an anesthesiologist to do it."

---

36 The Anschutz Entertainment Group (AEG) (also known as AEG Worldwide) is an American worldwide sporting and music entertainment presenter. Under the AEG Presents brand, it is the world's second largest presenter of live music and entertainment events after Live Nation.

Cherilyn is now disturbed. "I won't. It's unsafe. Any doctor agreeing to give you propofol at home doesn't care about you. They'll be doing it only for the money."

April 2009: A done deal

One day, at 04:30 AM, an agitated Michael stood up from his bed after four hours of night sleep. He stared at Cherilyn with his big brown eyes and said, "I told you I cannot sleep all night. I've got to get my sleep so I can do this."

A few hours later, he called Dr Conrad Murray, his personal physician.

Michael: Have you found somebody?

Conrad: They all rejected the offer, Michael.

Michael: Not a single anesthesiologist?

Conrad: Not a single one

Michael: You have to do it yourself, then. Please, Conrad. This is a life saver for me.

****

This was the subject of the email sent by an AEG Live executive:

Dr Conrad Murray was hired for $150,000 a month to serve as Jackson's full-time physician.

The effect of propofol is magical. Michael is at his best form now, doing his 360 degrees spin more brilliant than he has ever been. It is a joy and an enormous relief to all at the rehearsals.

Jackson has been infused with propofol every night for the next 60 days, never happened to any human being before him.

June 2009: Trouble on the front

"Is he still not sleeping? Conrad told me he now sleeps like a baby; calm, deep and long."

"Yes, indeed. No issues with sleeping now. We don't know what's wrong with him."

Jackson is becoming progressively thinner and paranoid. He is talking to himself, and repeatedly saying that "God is talking to me." Moreover, he is struggling to grasp work at rehearsals, needing psychiatric help. He now needs a teleprompter[37] to memorize the lyrics he has sung thousands of times before over many decades. On one occasion, he has had severe chills on a summer day in Los Angeles, with his skin as cold as ice to the touch.

An e-mail chain—titled "Trouble at the Front"—is exchanged between AEG live managers six days before the death of Michael Jackson:

"I have watched him deteriorate in front of my eyes over the last eight weeks. He was able to do multiple 360 spins back in April. He'd fall on his ass if he tried now," production manager John "Bugzee" Houghdahl wrote, expressing his concerns in correspondence to AEG Live CEO Randy Phillips on June 19, 2009.

Show director Kenny Ortega sent Jackson home from a rehearsal that night because of his strange behavior.

------

37 Also known as an autocue, a display device that prompts the person speaking with an electronic visual text of a speech or script.

"He was a basket case[38] and Kenny was concerned he would embarrass himself on stage, or worse yet—get hurt," Houghdahl commented. "The company is rehearsing right now, but the DOUBT is pervasive."

Four years later: His eyes could not dance

Dr Charles Czeisler is a Harvard Medical School sleep expert who was consulted by the Portland Trail blazers[39] after they lost a series of East Coast basketball matches. He gave their players strategies for being sharper when traveling across time zones.

He has also assisted the Rolling Stones[40] with their sleep problems. In addition, Dr Czeisler has developed a program for NASA to manage astronauts' sleep in space, where they have a sunrise and sunset every 90 minutes. In addition, he provided the CIA, the Secret Service, and the U.S. Air Force with his expertise to solve issues related to night shifts.

Now, Dr Czeisler is in a Los Angeles courtroom to explain what happened to Michael Jackson during the last 60 days of his life:

"Propofol disrupts the normal sleep cycle and offers no rapid eye movement (REM) sleep, which is vital to keep the brain and body alive. Yet, it leaves a patient feeling refreshed as if they had experienced genuine sleep, but without the benefits that genuine sleep delivers in repairing brain cells and the body.

---

38 A person or thing regarded as useless or unable to cope.

39 An American professional basketball team based in Portland, Oregon. They compete in the National Basketball Association (NBA).

40 An English rock band formed in London in 1962. Their estimated record sales of 240 million makes them one of the best-selling music artists of all time. In 2019, Billboard magazine ranked them second in their list of the "Greatest Artists of All Time" based on US chart success.

It would be like eating some sort of cellulose pellets instead of dinner. Your stomach would be full, and you would not be hungry, but it would be zero calories and not fulfill any of your nutrition needs."

"If he had not died on June 25, 2009, of an overdose of the surgical anesthetic, the lack of REM sleep may have taken his life within days anyway. Lab rats die after five weeks of getting no REM sleep. Translating that to a human, Jackson would have died before his 80th day of propofol infusions."

"Your brain needs sleep to repair and maintain its neurons every night. Blood cells cycle out every few weeks, but brain cells are for a lifetime. Like a computer, the brain has to go offline to maintain cells that we keep for life, since we don't make more. Sleep is the repair and maintenance of the brain cells. An adult should get seven to eight hours of sleep each night to allow for enough sleep cycles.

You 'prune out' unimportant neuron connections and consolidate important ones during your "slow-eyed sleep" each night. Those connections—which is the information you have acquired during the day—are consolidated by the REM sleep cycle. Your eyes actually dart back and forth rapidly during REM sleep.

In REM, we are integrating the memories that we have stored during slow-eyed sleep, integrating memories with previous life experiences. We are able to make sense of things that we may not have understood while awake. Learning and memory happen when you are asleep. A laboratory mouse rehearses a path through a maze to get to a piece of cheese while asleep. The area of a basketball player's brain that is used to shoot a ball will have much greater slow-eyed sleep period since there is more for it to store, he said. Players shoot better after sleep."

"Depriving someone of REM sleep for a long period of time makes them paranoid, anxiety-filled, depressed, unable to learn, distracted and sloppy. They lose their balance and appetite while their physical reflexes get 10 times slower and their emotional responses 10 times stronger."

"These manifestations are analogous to symptoms documented by e-mails among show producers and testimony from Michael's chef, hairstylist and choreographers including his inability to do standard dances or remember words to songs he sang for decades, paranoia, talking to himself and hearing voices in addition severe weight loss."

A truly sad story and a tragic end to a legend, but there is a lot to be learnt from it.

References: 27, 81-86.

Stages of Sleep

- There are four sleep stages that keep on repeating all night: one for rapid eye movement (REM) sleep and three that form non-REM (NREM) sleep.

- These stages are determined based on an analysis of brain activity during sleep.

- Stage 1   NREM N1   1-5 minutes (Dozing off – Easy to be woken up.)

- Stage 2   NREM N2   10-60 minutes (Gets longer overnight, 50% of sleep time.)

- Stage 3   NREM N3   20-40 minutes (Slow wave, deep sleep—Gets shorter in the second half of the night—restorative sleep, allowing for recovery, repair, growth and boosting the immune system. There is evidence of contribution to insightful thinking, creativity, and memory. Difficult to be woken up.)

- Stage 4   REM   10-60 minutes (Paralysis of all muscles, except for the eyes and muscles of breathing. Important for memory, learning, and creativity. Known for the most vivid dreams, which can happen in any stage, but more common and intense here. Gets longer in the second half of the night.)

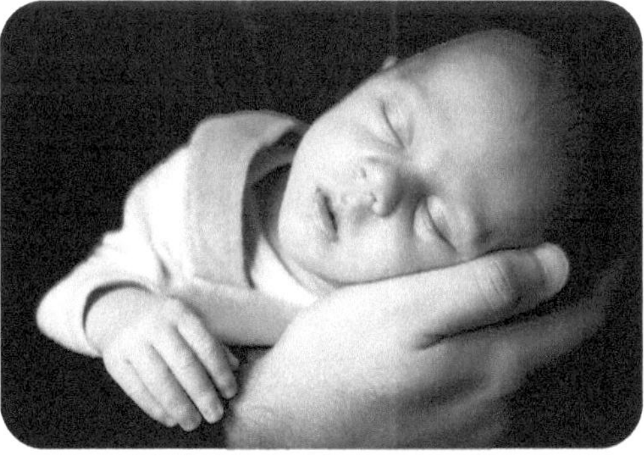

Reference: 87

A 2020 SLEEPING BEAUTY

Lujain:

Don't think that the Covid-19 virus thing has been completely bad. True, it has taken my mum from me, but it has made me such a smart person. Now, I see better, I hear better, and understand far, far better.

At the moment, I can see the evil of my grand mum Lina as I've never seen it before. The full abilities I now have saved my life on many occasions. Half asleep, I can hear her reading her dreadful black magic scripts and spells beside my bed. I have been wondering all my life how a lady of her age doesn't sleep at all. Midnight she is there, 2 AM she is awake, 4 AM she is up. Active all day. I figured it must be due to her satanic powers.

She doesn't know that I spotted her once at 5 AM, wearing her hoodie, mask, and gloves, gliding outside the house in the dark. She was carrying this bucket full of her malicious potions to spray all over the neighborhood.

I was locked in the house 24/7. She banned my best friend and neighbor Seema from visiting. She even banned my tutor, Ben, from coming! Ruining my life is her ultimate goal.

The most horrible thing this scrooge does is emptying the fridge. Have you ever heard of something like that? A supposedly loving, caring grandma adopting a miserable grieving adolescent girl who lost her parents, then she empties the fridge every afternoon to save the money of feeding her!!! How horrible!!!

I feel like I'm floating into space again. It must be one of her wicked potions.

***

Ben picked the phone.

"Hi, it's Seema."

"Hi, love."

"Hi, Ben. We need to do something for Lujain. We can't leave her locked in by this old witch. Can we?"

"No. But the issue is Luji's sleeping all the time. She is barely awake. To move her out, we need her to join with us. Otherwise, it will look like kidnap."

"True. But this witch is doping her with these potions all the time. What should we do?"

"The police? Doctors?"

"I don't think they will help. She's a *witch*, Ben. Have you seen the police arresting witches before? Have you ever seen doctors specialized in treating spells, potions, and black magic? We'll get into trouble without gaining anything. Believe me. Best case scenario, she'll turn the tables and say nasty things about us and worst case, she'll curse us with a spell."

"Let me think of a plan."

***

Lina:

I was called to the police station today. As if I needed another pain in the neck. I had to meet a sergeant called Zane.

"Is this a formal investigation?" I asked him.

"Not yet, Mrs. Hedar. Not at this stage," he answered.

"Why not?" I queried.

"Because we don't have anything official yet; no official accusations. Just gossip from here and there. We'd like to be preemptive and get on top of things before it gets out of hand," he replied.

"Wonderful. Our police now have plenty of free time to tackle gossips."

He didn't seem to enjoy my sarcasm and pulled a serious face.

"Well, Mrs. Hedar, about your granddaughter, Lujain. To be honest, we received an anonymous call concerned about her wellbeing."

I responded, "My grand-daughter Lujain is ill. A few months ago, she had coronavirus, which also killed her mother. Since then, she had not been herself; sleeping all the time, having hallucinations and delusions, eating a lot, being fearful and childish, missed school and her part-time job. I'm the only one looking after her. She has a condition."

"What sort of condition?" he asked.

"Sleeping beauty disease."

With a laugh, Zane queried cynically: "Sleeping beauty??!! Is that a real disease?"

"Well. You can google it."

"Which doctor is looking after her? Is she taking medicines?"

"A doctor in the city, in La Familia Hospital. The head of the department there. I don't remember his name. Of course, I'm giving her medicines," I replied.

"So, you are not locking her down?" his never-ending questions continued.

"I am indeed. I am telling you that she has hallucinations and delusions. She is fearful and her behavior is childish. It is not safe for her to wander on her own, and I am too old to supervise her if we go out together."

"But you are also banning her friend and her tutor," Sergeant Zane commented.

"Ah, now I know who your anonymous caller is. They were having sex in her room."

The surprised sergeant asked:" Who?"

"Ben and Seema. They were having sex in her room. I wouldn't allow a threesome in my ill granddaughter's room."

Finally, he gave up on me. "OK. Mrs. Hedar," he sighed. "Please just be careful. We'll be watching ... and helping as well if you need support."

***

Lujain:

"What is this?" I asked the evil old woman.

"The sheep brain you asked for," she answered with a yellow smile.

"Brrrrrrrrrrain?!! That's disgusting!"

"I thought so and I was astonished you requested it yesterday," she needled me.

This woman wanted to make me feel mad. So I won't let her. "OK. I'll take it."

Stunned, she responded, "I thought you said it is disgusting." The look at her face was priceless.

I took the brain to my room. It smelled of poison. I thought of throwing it in the toilet. Yet, on a second thought, I called the police.

***

As soon as the police arrested Lina Hedar, Ben and Seema decided to enter the house.

Lujain was deeply asleep in her bed as usual. Ben started looking around, scanning the door, the window, the obstacles to the way out and Lujain's position, thinking of the most practical technicalities involved in moving the miserable teenager out. But Seema was looking elsewhere, opening the cupboard and the drawers. She started collecting things in a big handbag she was holding.

"What are you doing?" wondered Ben.

Seema answered in rush, panting, "Keeping the valuables safe for her. Many people will be in and out this house in the coming couple of weeks."

"Let's focus on her first. She is the most valuable here. After moving her out, we can come back later to do this," responded Ben with concern.

"Why do you want to move her out now?" Seema asked, stopping her search.

"What? I thought that's why we're here?" Ben said with more concern.

Seema trying to be rational. "Listen. The ambulance and social services will be here any time now. Do you think the authorities will leave her lying down alone in the house like that? She is already safe in their hands. As long as this woman is imprisoned, she'll be all right."

Ben was now perplexed. "But you told me few days ago that there are no doctors specialized in treating spells, potions, and black magic. Remember? Can't you see her? We've been making noise for some time now and she hasn't even moved a fingertip, not a flicker."

Seema was fed up. "Come oooon, Ben! There's no such thing. She is *not* cursed. She has a condition; a medical problem."

"A condition??!! You knew that all the time??!! Why have you been spreading these witch and magic rumors then??!!" a baffled Ben questioned her.

Seema mumbled, embarrassed, "It came from Luji herself. I took it from her and spread it after that nasty woman caught us romping here and humiliated us."

"I'm not with you on this anymore. I'm leaving. This is terrible."

Furious, Ben left at once. A few minutes later, the ambulance and social services arrived at the house. Seema managed to hide in the storage cabinet, so that she could accomplish her mission after their departure.

***

At his office, Sergeant Zane welcomed his unexpected visitor.

"I am Dr Serhan Halilovich," the visitor said, "the Head of the Department of Psychiatry at La Familia Hospital.

The police officer encouraged the psychiatrist to open up about his testimony.

Dr Halilovich started, "Yes. There is a disease with that name—Sleeping Beauty syndrome—and there is no beauty in it. In medical terms, we call it Kleine–Levin syndrome. Miss Lujain Hedar is suffering from it."

"Never heard of it," Sergeant Zane replied.

"It affects only one in a million following viral infections. Unfortunately, Lujain had it after she caught Covid-19. Patients like her sleep in episodes for long hours; up to 21 hours per day. They eat a lot while they are awake and get overweight. That's why I advised Lujain's grandmother to make sure the fridge is emptied regularly of excess food."

"Do sufferers ask for foods unusual in their culture, like brains?" Zane enquired.

"Exactly," Dr Halilovich confirmed. "They sometimes also get delusions and hallucinations in relation to vision, hearing, smell, and taste. Occasionally, they lose their sense of reality. Sometimes, they are fearful and act in a childish manner."

"Poor kid. Is it a lifelong condition?"

"No. But it stays for many years, 10-12-13 maybe. Each episode lasts for several days or weeks. They are more or less normal in between the episodes. For Lujain's case, it is a bit more complicated because of the impressions and concepts she has built up due to her hallucinations and delusions, which make it difficult for her to be 100% normal in between the episodes."

"Thanks for your help with such complicated case, Doctor."

***

As Lina walked free from the police station, a voice called from behind her.

She looked over her shoulder to find a welcoming smile.

"Congrats," said Dr Halilovich.

She returned the kind smile. "Thanks."

"Are you still awake for 21 hours per day?"

"Of course," Lina replied. "I have this gene, you know."

"Yes. The DEC2[41]."

"Isn't it weird that I have a condition keeping me awake for 21 hours a day, while my granddaughter has a condition that keeps her asleep for 21 hours a day??!!!"

Dr Halilovich laughed. "It is indeed."

They both looked up as Sergeant Zane appeared, calling Lina. As he approached them, he handed over an envelope to her.

"This is your car washing money," he said.

"You mean, for my bucket of potions," she responded with a smile.

Zane explained to Halilovich, "Lujain used to wash the neighborhood cars before her illness as a spare time job. When she fell ill, Lina decided to carry on with Lujain's car washing in the early hours of the morning, without telling anybody. She didn't want the neighbors to feel any change and she didn't want her granddaughter to be replaced, hoping that she'll do that again once she recovers."

With admiring eyes, Dr Halilovich asked Lina, "Would you like me to drop you home?"

"I'd be grateful for that. I need some rest before visiting Lujain in the hospital. I need to bring over her books to read the lessons she missed," replied Lina.

---

41 In 2009, researchers in the University of California at San Francisco, led by Professor Ying-Hui Fu discovered that mutations of the DEC2 gene are responsible for a rare pattern of short sleep. People affected sleep for much fewer hours than the expected seven to eight hours required for healthy humans, without suffering with any adverse health effects.

"Is there any point in doing that? Will she take in any knowledge from your reading? Will she appreciate it?" asked Zane.

Lina responded confidently, "Not in my lifetime. But I am sure you'll find an opportunity to tell her one day when she is back to her normal self. Let's go, Doctor."

Extremes of Dreamland

❯ There are medical conditions causing hypersomnia other than the "Sleeping Beauty syndrome". Some of them are genetic, such as Prader-Willi syndrome, Norrie disease, and Niemann–Pick disease, type C.

❯ Head trauma, brain tumors, Parkinson's disease, Alzheimer's, obesity, and depression may also cause hypersomnia.

❯ In 1959, UK hypnotist Peter Powers put himself under a hypnotic sleep for eight straight days. It made a big splash in the media, although it doesn't quite count as sleeping.

❯ In October 2017, Wyatt Shaw from Kentucky fell asleep for 11 days. He was just seven years old and no conclusive explanations were found despite thorough investigations into the incident. He woke up with cognitive impairment but fully recovered with epilepsy medications.

❯ In addition to the DEC2 gene mutation causing short sleep pattern discovered in 2009, two more gene mutations for people who have short sleep pattern have been revealed more recently: the ADRB1 gene and NPSR1 gene, both discovered in 2019.

❯ In 1959, Peter Tripp stayed awake for 201 hours i.e. 8.4 days straight. However, he suffered from hallucinations and paranoia afterwards.

❯ Randy Gardener, at the age of 17, remained awake for 11 straight days and broke the world record for the longest time without sleep. He made the record in 1964 and still holds it as of 2020.

❯ The Guinness World Records stopped supervising and reviewing such attempts for fear of health hazards.

References: *27, 88-93.*

A BLOODY NIGHT IN DREAMLAND

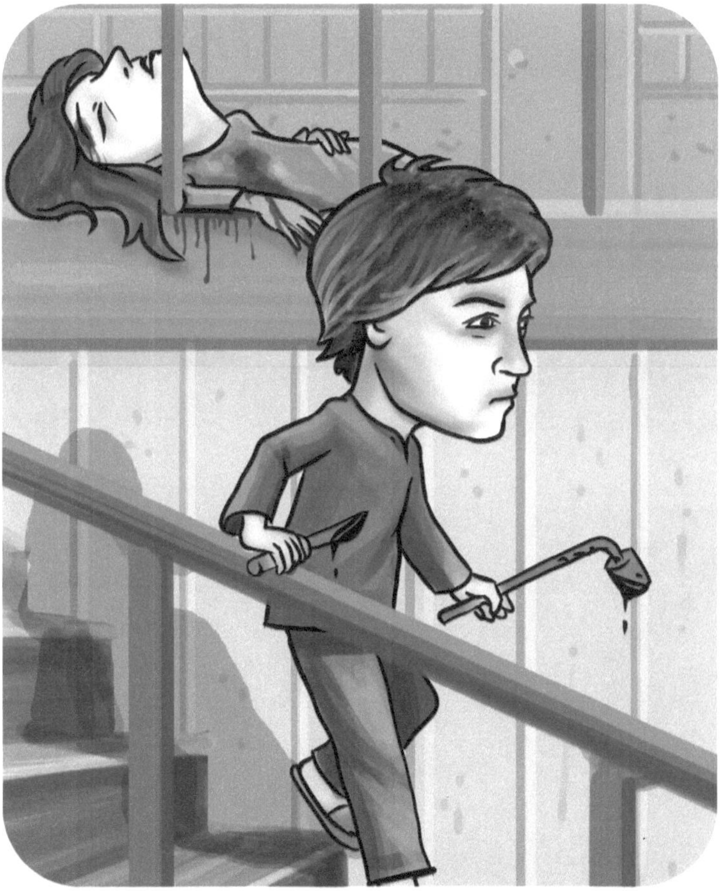

Kenneth fetched the tire iron from his car trunk and walked steadily but slowly towards his in-law's house. He took the key out of his pocket.

After grabbing a knife from the kitchen, he advanced upstairs.

Suspicious about the footsteps outside her bedroom, Barbara came out. There was no time for surprise in response to the sudden appearance of her gentle giant son-in-law as she used to call him. He bludgeoned her with the tire iron and followed with eight stabs with the knife. His father-in-law, Dennis, who rushed to see what was happening, was stabbed as well then choked until he lost consciousness.

Back in the kitchen, Kenneth picked up the phone and set it down again, off the hook. He ran upstairs to his sister-in-laws' bedrooms. However, he halted at the doors, rushed downstairs again and left the house, headed towards the police station. He arrived at 4:45 AM, covered in blood, shaking, and severely distressed. He did not seem to be in pain, despite having cut tendons in both hands. He said:

"I just killed someone with my bare hands; oh my God, I just killed someone; I've just killed two people; my God, I've just killed two people with my hands; my God, I've just killed two people. My hands; I just killed two people. I killed them; I just killed two people; I've just killed my mother– and father-in-law. I stabbed and beat them to death. It's all my fault."

Arrested for the first-degree murder of Barbara Ann Woods and the attempted murder of her husband, 23-year-old Kenneth James Parks seemed destined for conviction and life imprisonment. Yet, the May 1987 crime that shook the Toronto suburb of Scarborough twisted into the weirdest possible scenario during the trial. "Kenneth James Parks cannot be held liable for his actions because he committed them while sleepwalking," claimed the defense attorney. "What? You mean somnambulism[42]?" the astonished prosecution asked.

"Yes. Exactly," answered Kenneth's lawyer with a calm smile. He added, "Kenneth's mother told me that, when he was 13 to 14 years old, she went in to check on him and his legs were going out the 6th-floor window. Kenneth's grandfather was also a sleepwalker. He would walk around in the house and sometimes cook food without eating it.

Sir, on that tragic night last May, Kenneth was talking with his wife about fixing his in-law's furnace. Shortly afterwards, his wife went up to bed, while Kenneth fell asleep on the couch. It suddenly came to Kenneth in his sleep that he should fix his in-law's furnace. He got up and drove to the house but was startled by his in-laws. He attacked both of them without knowing what he was doing. His next recollection was seeing his mother-in-law's face with her eyes and mouth open. Kenneth described it as a very sad face. After seeing Barbara's face, he heard the kids screaming. He remembers thinking the kids were in trouble and needed help. He yelled 'kids, kids, kids!' and went upstairs. Actually, the kids didn't hear him yell. They heard only grunting noises of the sort made by a person during sleep.

---

42 A twilight state between sleep and wakefulness during which sleepers could engage in complex activities. Examples include: carrying on phantom conversations, wandering around, eating, or even potentially dangerous activities such as swimming or driving.

Police officers reported that Kenneth was not feeling any pain in his hands despite his injuries. This is what specialists call dissociative analgesia. It occurs during sleepwalking. Kenneth is ready to be examined and tested by experts to verify these facts."

The defense claims were met with skepticism and even ridicule at all levels.

The prosecution attempted to invalidate them with nullifying facts:

- Kenneth had severe financial trouble due to a gambling addiction.

- He stole $32,000 from his employer Revere Electric, for which he was fired and court proceedings were brought against him just two months before the incident.

- On his way to his in-law's house, he drove 23 km, crossing many intersections, which is too complicated to maneuver while asleep.

- Kenneth's wife has never seen him sleepwalking, only talking to her whilst asleep.

- Kenneth's relatives who experienced sleepwalking included his grandfather who never left the house when sleepwalking. His sleepwalking cousin left the house during her sleepwalking, but just sat outside. None went on long trips or ended up carrying out highly complex actions requiring conscious control.

- The police reported signs of a great struggle in the bedroom: "The bed was disheveled, the pillows were soaked in blood, and the mattress was moved around so that the headboard was tipped forward." It is implausible that such struggle, them screaming at him, asking him what he was doing, imploring with him, failed to wake him up.

Surprisingly, after robust expert testing and analysis, the experts could find no other explanation of the crime than sleepwalking. The electroencephalography (EEG)[43] scans confirmed that Kenneth had some abnormal brain activity during deep sleep and periods of partial awakenings, diagnosed as parasomnia[44]. Faking EEG results is not possible.

Kenneth was acquitted and walked free from the court. The supreme court upheld the decision. Since then, he has taken medications for his sleep problems, never sleepwalked again, and never committed any more crimes. His life has been transferred for the better.

Nonetheless, this case is marked as a historical milestone in Canada and the whole world, from both the legal and psychological perspective. More than three decades after the closure of the trial, the debate is still raging.

From the legal perspective, sleepwalking does not automatically guarantee full acquittal. If Kenneth or any offender in his situation has a pre-existent "disease of the mind" causing him to be insane during the offence, he is not entitled for full acquittal, even if the deed was involuntary.

"Disease of the mind" is a legal—not medical—term, to enable the judge to bypass the medical opinion if there is a motive and the act is likely to recur. A condition likely to present recurring danger should be treated as insanity. If the build up to the crime is triggered only and fully by the criminal's mind rather than external factors, complete acquittal is not applicable.

---

43   An electrophysiological monitoring method to record electrical activity of the brain. It is typically noninvasive, with the electrodes placed along the scalp.

44   A category of sleep disorders involving abnormal movements, behaviors, emotions, perceptions, and dreams that occur while falling asleep, sleeping, between sleep stages, or during arousal from sleep.

The defense in Kenneth's case argued that the killing was triggered by a compilation of external factors that are unlikely to recur. Yet, there is a strong argument that due to temporary insanity, Kenneth was not fully in control of his actions, although he might have been conscious of them. In other words, voluntary but unintentional.

From the medical perspective, sleep scientists are still asking an important question:

Was Kenneth truly fully asleep all the time, or could he have been conscious at least for some time but repressed the dreadful memories instantly?

Many experts are convinced of the latter. Sleepwalking occurs in the deep stage of sleep with the emergence of slow brain waves. During this stage, people who are asleep are not conscious of sensory input from their surroundings. During sleep, there is also a gating mechanism blocking input from the cognitive brain to the muscles.

Nevertheless, in parasomnia, there is a defect in this gating mechanism that allows substantial input to the muscles. Thus, the brain can command the muscles during sleep. Also, sleepwalkers have their eyes open: They can see their surroundings but not consciously. Basically, sleepwalkers are awake and asleep at the same time.

Sleepwalkers can only complete tasks they have done many times before; incorporated in their minds as routine. That is, only tasks that do not require thinking and cognition. Often sleepwalkers get hurt while travelling on holidays as they are not familiar with the new environment. In 2007, Canadian tennis player Peter Polansky broke the window of his hotel room in Mexico then fell down through the broken glass while sleepwalking.

The more complex the acts of the criminal are, the less likely it is that they were done during a full sleepwalking state. The evidence for that comes from real, non-criminal stories of sleepwalking people, who are unable to do such acts. Often the defense is clever enough to use the excuse of sleepwalking to acquit their defendants.

If you are driving and lost your concentration for a while, you will miss exits and turns. If you do not focus on your route, you will find yourself subconsciously on a route familiar to you rather than your intended navigation. It is extremely illogical to believe that some-body can drive through an unfamiliar route with no accidents while sleepwalking. This was the case for Kenneth who has not visited his in-law's house for at least two months before the tragedy.

The possibility of Kenneth having hallucinations during the atrocity has been also raised. He said that he yelled "kids, kids, kids" after hearing his sisters-in-law screaming. The girls' account of the incident was different. They said he was only grunting in the way some asleep people do, without saying anything. Therefore, it is very possible that Parks' account resulted from hallucinations rather than an attempt to mislead the jury.

Unless we can have a tool capable of monitoring brain activity precisely in real-time during such crimes, or at least to provide the ability to retrieve it, absolute justice in such grey accountabilities will continue to be remote. Such technology is currently a science fiction commodity. However, artificial intelligence was in the same category that night that Kenneth entered his in-law's house for the last time, and things have certainly progressed in that area.

References: 94-97.

Other Dreamland Killings

- Boshears' case: Sergeant Willis Boshears, a US serviceman based in the UK, confessed to strangling a local woman named Jean Constable in the early hours on New Year's Day 1961. At his trial, he pled not guilty on the basis of being asleep at the time he committed the offence and was acquitted.

- Falater's case: Scott Falater from Phoenix, Arizona murdered his wife, Yarmila, by stabbing her 44 times on January 16, 1997. The prosecution proved that after the murder, Falater changed his clothes, placed the weapon in a Tupperware container, put the container in a trash bag, and then hid the bag in the spare tire well in the trunk of his car; "too complex" to have been carried out while sleepwalking. Falater was convicted of first-degree murder and sentenced to life in prison without the possibility of parole.

- Nieto's case: Antonio Nieto, 58, from Málaga, Spain killed his wife and mother-in-law using an axe and a hammer on January 11, 2001. His daughter suffered a jaw fracture and his son disarmed him after receiving a cut on the ear. Nieto claimed to have been asleep and dreaming of defending himself against aggressive ostriches. However, his children stated that he had recognized them and had even asked his son to keep the lights off as his mother was sleeping. Nieto was sentenced to 10 years confinement in a psychiatric hospital and ordered to pay 171,100 euros as compensation to the victims.

- Lowe's case: On October 30, 2004, the body of 83-year-old Edward Lowe was discovered on his driveway in Manchester, England. His son, Jules, admitted that he caused his father's death, but did not remember committing the act and used "automatism" as his defense. He was found not guilty by reason of insanity and detained at Her Majesty's pleasure (supposedly indefinitely) in a secure hospital. He was freed after 10 months.

- ◢ Brian Thomas' case: Brian Thomas, 59, who had a history of sleep-walking since childhood, confessed to strangling his 57-year old wife, Christine, in July 2008 in their van while on holiday. He called emergency services: "What have I done? I've been trying to wake her. I think I've killed my wife. Oh my God. I thought someone had broken in. I was fighting with those boys, but it was Christine. I must have been dreaming or something. What have I done?" He claimed he had mistaken his wife for an intruder. He was found not guilty of murder and released in 2009.

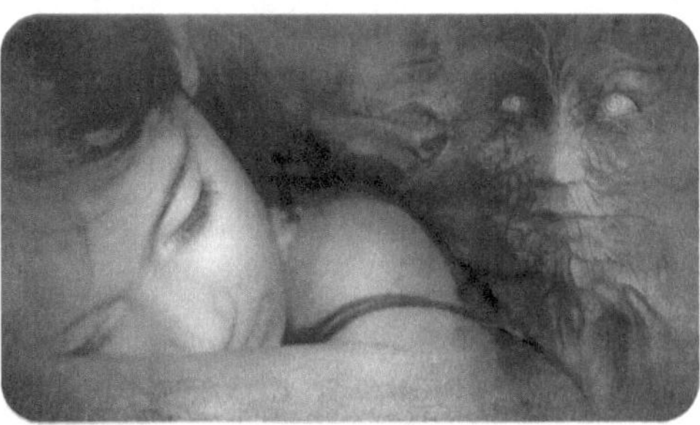

References: 27, 98-101.

SLUMBER ART

"Come on, Robert. He started!" shrieked Amber in excitement.

The eager psychiatrist left the tea kettle on and rushed to the TV screen. He sat by his colleague and they watched together.

As the video streamed, they were pretty amazed.

Their eyes kept on wandering between the video and the EEG monitor.

Both were keen to write their notes on what was going on.

It took Lee three hours to complete the portrait. He left his tools on the nearby table, went back to bed, and threw his duvet on.

At the end of the video, Amber looked to Robert. "Genuine?" she asked.

"Definitely", answered Robert as he sat back in his chair.

The next week, Amber and Robert had a meeting with Lee's parents. "He is certainly unique," started Robert.

"He can't draw, Doctor. His art work is horrific. One of the worst amongst his friends, always a D in Art classes," Lee's father replied, quite baffled. "But apparently, he is another person at night," Amber remarked. "It seems the talent kicks in while he's asleep. When did it all start, may I ask?"

"At four, he started to use his crayons and scribble on the walls in the middle of the night. As he grew up, his drawings became more and more intricate, only at night. We first thought he woke up to do it, but the specialists told us he was deeply asleep."

" True indeed," Amber replied. "Our studies have confirmed that."

"Any scientific explanations?" asked Lee's dad.

Puzzled, Robert shook his head. "Complete mystery, unfortunately. Did he have any trauma in the past?"

"Nope."

"My advice is to just let him carry on," Robert said, concluding the visit.

On their way to the door, Amber asked the parents, "Do you want him to grow out of it?"

The parents looked to each other. With a smile, Lee's mum replied, "Probably not."

Lee Hadwin, 45 at the time of publication, was born in Australia, but grew up in the UK.

He currently has solo shows of his artistic works, which you can explore on his website.

Lee used to be a care worker but has now become a full-time artist.

Donald Trump owns a piece of his artwork and the Marilyn Monroe museum in Hollywood bought three of his drawings for approximately $6,000. These were the first of his more complex portraits as a teenager. "I drew the Marilyn Monroe pictures and, in the morning, I just looked at them and thought 'Oh wow!'" he said.

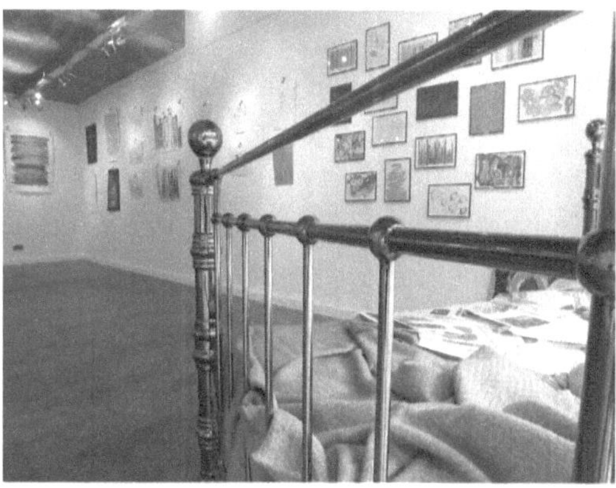

Over the next two decades, he produced more than 600 paintings in different styles.

In 2013, Lee gained thousands of pounds when he auctioned a large collection on eBay. He donated half the proceeds to The Missing People charity.

Initially, Hadwin was not welcomed by critics and trained artists, and still many of them don't recognize him as talented enough. Previously, he used to be upset by such views. Yet, more recently, he has started to be more pragmatic about it. He was taken on by the management team Incandescent Artists, has travelled on worldwide tours, and had his own exhibition, Hypnos. Whether people are buying his paintings due to distinction, brilliance, or out of curiosity, it does not matter. His works generally sell for between $1,500 and $10,000. He explains, "I never take it personally. At the end of the day, art is subjective, and it doesn't matter if you've studied art for one year or 40—if someone likes a piece, that's all that matters."

Lee's schedule is random. He may do two paintings a week or one in a couple of months, keeping his tools and materials nearby his bed to be prepared for the moment; such moments are by no means inspired by any thoughts or external factors he gets exposed to at bedtime.

Scientists believe sleepwalking occurs when two areas of the brain — the limbic system, which manages raw emotions and the cortex controlling complex motor activity remain conscious while the areas in charge of primitive impulses like the frontal cortex[45] (rationality) and hippocampus[46] (memory) sleep.

As in Lee's case, scientists currently agree that bouts of localized wakeful-like activity in the cortex and the limbic system may happen without concurrent sleepwalking.

Nevertheless, all of these explanations do not explain why people like Hadwin are so talented and creative only during night sleep, but

---

45　The outer layer of neural tissue of the brain in humans and other mammals. The two hemispheres are joined beneath the cortex by a body called the corpus callosum. The cortex is the largest site of neural integration in the central nervous system. It plays a key role in attention, perception, awareness, thought, memory, language, and consciousness.

46　A major component of the brain of humans and other vertebrates. Humans and other mammals have two hippocampi, one in each side. It plays important roles in the consolidation of information from short-term memory to long-term memory, and in spatial memory that enables navigation.

perform so awfully in the same tasks during daytime. This is not just about emotions and motor activity.

A piece of the puzzle could be that there are published reports of non-professional artists who started practicing visual art only after the occurrence of brain damage from a stroke, degenerative brain disease[47], or head injury. (That's why Lee's parents were asked if he had trauma prior to the start of his phenomenon.) Yet, those artists show their talent all the time, not only during sleep.

Scientific analysis of de novo talent patients—especially related to painting and drawing—after brain damage has led to a couple of theories about this bizarre outcome:

(1) diminished inhibition of expression that normally exerts control over the cortex.

(2) A depletion in one or more of the brain neurotransmitters that resets the balance between these chemicals, creating new pathways of expression. (In the case of Parkinson's disease, Dopamine is depleted).

Further, drawing and painting are particularly linked to a large brain network called the salience network. Any change in such talents must be due to a change in this network.

As the variation to Lee Hadwin's artistic abilities is not persistent, probably there is still an unproven change to his brain chemicals and pathways that occurs only during sleep then gets reverted as he wakes up.

---

47 Include Parkinson's disease, Alzheimer's, and others. Occur as a result of neurodegenerative processes, which lead to the progressive loss of structure or function of neurons, including death of neurons. Such diseases are currently incurable.

The scientific discovery of why and how this change happens will widely open the door to a gigantic treasure of talents if they can be stimulated for many in the daytime, not just during their slumber.

____

References: 102-105.

Creepy Dreamlands

- Parasomnias are a category of sleep disorders involving abnormal movements, behaviors, emotions, perceptions, and dreams that occur while falling asleep, sleeping, between sleep stages, or during arousal from sleep.

- Confusional arousals: Confused state after waking up from sleep, sitting up to look around. Last anywhere from seconds to minutes and may not be reactive to stimuli. Lifetime prevalence of 18% in children and 4% in adults.

- Sleep-related abnormal sexual behavior (sexsomnia): A form of confusional arousal where a person will engage in sexual acts while still asleep. Unconscious, with clinical, social, and legal implications. A lifetime prevalence of 7%.

- Sleepwalking: A prevalence of 10% in childhood, with the most common occurrences around the age of 11-12. 4% of adults experience it. Anxiety, fatigue, alcohol, sedatives, medications, medical conditions, and mental disorders are all linked. May be associated with sleep talking.

- Sleep terrors (night terrors): The most disruptive as they may cause loud screams and panic, and in severe cases, bodily harm or property damage by running about or hitting walls. All attempts to comfort the individual are in vain. Usually the victim does not remember the incident. Up to 3% of adults are affected. Common in people with post-traumatic stress disorder (PTSD).

- Sleep-related eating disorder (SRED): High-caloric food is consumed in an uncontrolled manner. SRED should not be confused with nocturnal eating syndrome, which occurs in full consciousness.

- REM sleep behavior disorder: Most common in older adults who act out their dreams and may result in injuries to themselves or others. Patients should use self-protection measures by tethering themselves to bed, using pillow barricades, or sleeping in an empty room on a mattress. 90% are males, and most are older than 50 years of age.

- Recurrent isolated sleep paralysis: Inability to move voluntarily at sleep onset or on waking up. Although the person is conscious, they are unable to speak or move. Lasts for seconds to minutes and resolves spontaneously. The lifetime prevalence is 7%. Associated with sleep hallucinations. Sleep deprivation predisposes to it.

- Nightmare disorder: Recurrent nightmares associated with awakening sadness impairing the quality of life.

- Catathrenia: Breath holding and groaning during sleep. Like snoring, usually not felt by the person producing the sound but is very disturbing to sleep partner. But the sounds occur during exhalation rather than with inhalation which is characteristic of snoring.

- Sleep-Related Painful Erections: Affects men of all ages but more common from the middle-age.

- Sleep-related hallucinations: Brief episodes of dream-like imagery. Can be auditory, visual, or tactile.

- Sleep talking (somniloquy): An isolated symptom, which ranges from isolated speech to full conversations without recall. A lifetime prevalence of 69%

References: 27, 106-111.

15

DREAMS THAT CHANGED
THE WORLD

Modern human science and art owe vivid dreams a fortune. Let's read about one of these visionary dreams as described by the genius who lived it, Albert Einstein: "I was sledding with my friends at night. I started to slide down the hill but my sled started going faster and faster. I was going so fast that I realized I was approaching the speed of light. I looked up at that point and I saw the stars. They were being refracted into colors I had never seen before. I was filled with a sense of awe. I understood in some way that I was looking at the most important meaning in my life."

This was not Einstein's only dream on the matter of "relativity." In another fantasy, he had been hiking alongside a stream trickling from a snowy hill one misty morning, until he reached some cultivated fields separated by fences. He saw a small herd of cows clustering near an electric fence. As Einstein approached. a farmer appeared and activated the electric fence, horrifying the cows. The cows' reactions afterwards consumed the rest of the dream in a dispute between Einstein and the imaginary farmer. The scientist claimed that they all retreated at once, jumping simultaneously away from the fence, while the farmer argued that they moved away one after another. These were the sort of dreams occupying the mastermind of the theory that transformed physics and astronomy during the 20th century.

Einstein's sleep visions were not the only dreams that contributed to science milestones.

Niels Bohr, the father of quantum mechanics, repeatedly told the story of the inspiring dream that heralded the discovery of the structure of the atom.

Over a long time, Bohr worked on various configurations to reveal the structure of the atom, yet with no avail. One night, he went to bed and began to dream about atoms. He saw the nucleus, with electrons spinning around it, in the same way planets revolve around the sun. On waking up, Bohr followed the concept. He rushed to his lab and worked hard on the evidence to support his fantasy. Eventually, it was scientifically proven and turned out to be one of the greatest breakthroughs of the 20th century, and brought Niels a Nobel prize.

In 1845, Elias Howe was awarded the first US patent for a sewing machine using a lockstitch design. The story of the invention had been communicated in his family memoirs:

"He almost beggared himself before he discovered where the eye of the needle of the sewing machine should be located ... he might have failed altogether if he had not dreamed, he was building a sewing machine for a savage king in a strange country. Just as in his actual working experience, he was perplexed about the needle's eye. He thought the king gave him twenty-four hours in which to complete the machine and make it sew. If not finished in that time death was to be the punishment.

Howe worked and worked, and puzzled, and finally gave it up. Then he thought he was taken out to be executed. He noticed that the warriors carried spears that were pierced near the head. Instantly came the solution of the difficulty, and while the inventor was begging for time, he awoke. It was four o'clock in the morning. He jumped out of bed, ran to his workshop, and by 9, a needle with an eye at the point had been rudely modeled. After that it was easy. That is the true story of an important incident in the invention of the sewing machine."

Srinivasa Ramanujan, the prodigy of Mathematics who proved more than 3,000 theorems stated that the intuition for his work was frequently inspired by his dreams. This is an example in his own words:

"While asleep I had an unusual experience. There was a red screen formed by flowing blood as it were. I was observing it. Suddenly a hand began to write on the screen. I became all attention. That hand wrote a number of results in elliptic integrals. They stuck to my mind. As soon as I woke up, I committed them to writing ..."

German-born pharmacologist Otto Loewi dreamed in 1921 of an experiment proving that transmission of nerve impulses was chemical not electrical. He woke up, wrote what he dreamed of, and went back to bed. When he arose in the morning, he was unable to comprehend his midsleep handwriting; a very sad day indeed he spent. Blissfully, the same dream was repeated the following night. This time, his adrenaline was pouring optimally for the most comprehensible scribble. The discovery of acetylcholine[48] won Loewi a Nobel prize 13 years later.

By the 1860s, Dmitri Mendeleev had been already unsuccessfully trying for few years to reach the rational pattern for tabulating the chemical elements. One evening, he dozed off at his desk to visualize the full charting of elements in a dream:

"I saw in a dream a table were all the elements fell into place as required. Awakening, I immediately wrote it down on a piece of paper, only in one place did a correction seem necessary."

---

48 A chemical that functions in the brain and body of many types of animals (including humans) as a neurotransmitter—a chemical message released by nerve cells to send signals to other cells, such as neurons, muscle cells, and gland cells.

Reihen	Gruppe I. R^2O	Gruppe II. RO	Gruppe III. R^2O^3	Gruppe IV. RH^4 RO^2	Gruppe V. RH^3 R^2O^5	Gruppe VI. RH^2 RO^3	Gruppe VII. RH R^2O^7	Gruppe VIII. RO^4
1	H = 1							
2	Li = 7	Be = 9,4	B = 11	C = 12	N = 14	O = 16	F = 19	
3	Na = 23	Mg = 24	Al = 27,3	Si = 28	P = 31	S = 32	Cl = 35,5	
4	K = 39	Ca = 40	— = 44	?Ti = 48	V = 51	Cr = 52	Mn = 55	Fe = 56, Co = 59, Ni = 59, Cu = 63.
5	(Cu = 63)	Zn = 65	— = 68	— = 72	As = 75	Se = 78	Br = 80	
6	Rb = 85	Sr = 87	?Yt = 88	Zr = 90	Nb = 94	Mo = 96	— = 100	Ru = 104, Rh = 104, Pd = 106, Ag = 108.
7	(Ag = 108)	Cd = 112	In = 113	Sn = 118	Sb = 122	Te = 125	J = 127	
8	Cs = 133	Ba = 137	?Di = 138	?Ce = 140	—	—	—	— — — —
9	(—)	—	—	—	—	—	—	
10	—	—	?Er = 178	?La = 180	Ta = 182	W = 184	—	Os = 195, Ir = 197, Pt = 198, Au = 199.
11	(Au = 199)	Hg = 200	Tl = 204	Pb = 207	Bi = 208	—	—	
12	—	—	—	Th = 231	—	U = 240	—	— — — —

During his sleep, the scientist's subconscious brain had put together the messed-up information his conscious brain had been working on in an intensive yet disorganized manner.

In 1890, the German Chemical Society celebrated the achievements of its distinguished member, the organic chemist August Kekulé. During his speech before the society, August said: "I was sitting writing at my textbook but the work did not progress; my thoughts were elsewhere. I turned my chair to the fire and dozed off. Again, the atoms were gamboling before my eyes. This time the smaller groups kept modestly in the background. My mental eye, rendered more acute by the repeated visions of the kind, could now distinguish larger structures of manifold confirmation: long rows, sometimes more closely fitted together all twining and twisting in snake like motion.

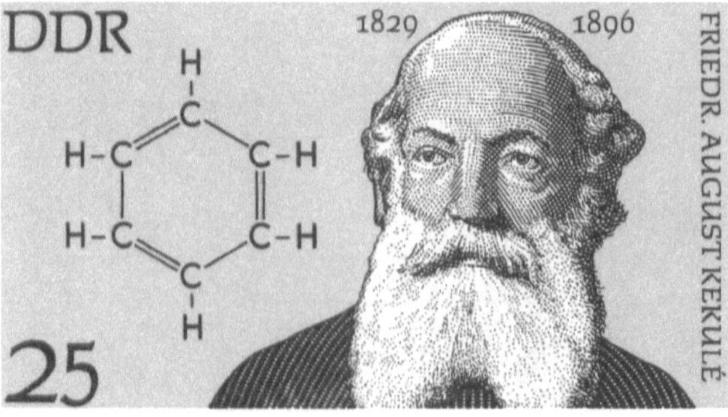

But look! What was that? One of the snakes had seized hold of its own tail, and the form whirled mockingly before my eyes. As if by a flash of lightning I awoke; and this time also I spent the rest of the night in working out the rest of the hypothesis."

This hypothesis discovered the ring shape of the Benzene molecule and provided new understanding of all aromatic compounds.

Fredrick Banting was not a diabetes specialist and he was not a researcher. However, he made one of the most remarkable advances in treatment of diabetes, if not the most remarkable of all. As his mother died of diabetes, Fredrick desperately sought the exact cause of the disease. Then he had a dream where he surgically tied up the pancreas of a diabetic dog. He did the same in real life and discovered an imbalance between sugar and insulin. In another dream, Banting learnt to use insulin to treat the condition. Not only did Banting become the youngest ever Nobel prize winner in Medicine at the age of 32, but more notably, he received the honor of hundreds of letters and gifts of gratitude from diabetic patients all over the world, and saved the lives of millions of people through the renowned treatment.

***

Interestingly, the Arts have been as fortunate as the Sciences in terms of benefits from sweet dreams.

One day in 1965, Paul McCartney rose with the full melody of the hit song "Yesterday" composed in his head. Instantly, he played it on his piano. But he had strong suspicion it was a sort of "cryptomnesia[49]". So, he started checking with his friends and family to see whether they'd ever heard it before:

"For about a month I went round to people in the music business and asked them whether they had ever heard it before. Eventually it became like handing something in to the police. I thought if no-one claimed it after a few weeks then I could have it."

---

49 Cryptomnesia occurs when a forgotten memory returns without its being recognized as such by the subject, who believes it is something new and original. It is a memory bias whereby a person may falsely recall generating a thought, an idea, a tune, a name, or a joke, not deliberately engaging in plagiarism but rather experiencing a memory as if it were a new inspiration.

He joined Lennon to write the lyrics and the song was credited to Lennon-McCartney on their album *Help!*. Yesterday remained at number one on the Billboard Hot 100 chart for four weeks. More than 2,200 cover versions have been made by other artists including Aretha Franklin, Katy Perry, The Mamas and the Papas, Michael Bolton, Bob Dylan, Ray Charles, Elvis Presley, and Billy Dean.

Mary Shelley is the author of the world's first science fiction novel, Frankenstein, and yet again, there was a vivid dream behind it. She was still a teenager when invited by the great English poet Lord Byron to his residence by Lake Geneva in Switzerland. The volcanic eruption of Mount Tambora locked them down. Byron suggested that they should kill time by writing a ghost story each. Mary tried hard with no luck, until the night when she dreamt what she describes here:

"I saw the pale student of unhallowed arts kneeling beside the thing he had put together. I saw the hideous phantasm of a man stretched out, and then, on the working of some powerful engine, show signs of life, and stir with an uneasy, half vital motion. Frightful must it be; for supremely frightful would be the effect of any human endeavor to mock the stupendous mechanism of the Creator of the world."

The Strange Case of Dr Jekyll and Mr. Hyde, written by Robert Louis Stevenson, does not lack fame, but the dreams behind it do:

"For two days I went about racking my brains for a plot of any sort; and on the second night I dreamed the scene at the window, and a scene afterward split in two, in which Hyde, pursued for some crime, took the powder and underwent the change in the presence of his pursuers."

One night Robert's wife Fanny heard his screams produced by an opium-induced nightmare. She rushed to wake him up, but he did not take it as a favor:

"Why did you wake me? I was dreaming a fine bogey tale."

Later on, Fanny found out that she had woken him at the first transformation scene. Within three days, Stevenson had written a 30,000-word draft.

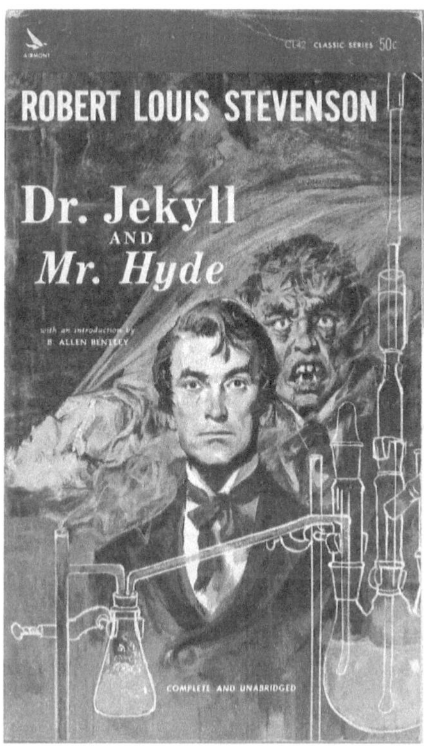

The titular character in *The Terminator* movie tickled the mind of director James Cameron in a dream he had while sick with fever. A shiny character of doom emerged from fire; a metallic monster with red eyes, dragging itself on the floor with kitchen knives:

"I was sick and dead broke in Rome, Italy, with a fever of 102, doing the final cut of *Piranha II*. That's when I thought of Terminator. I guess it was a fever dream."

Were all of these dream inspirations of divine origin, just lucky coincidences, or products or maybe by-products of waking minds consolidated by the sleeping brain?

The next chapter will try to answer this dilemma.

Dreamland Myths

- ↘ Your body gets used to less sleep: Continuous sleep deprivation impairs decision-making, memory, focus, and creativity. In the longer term, it adversely affects your metabolism, the cardiovascular system, the immune system, hormone production, and mental health. Even if you feel like you are adapting to shorter sleep, health problems may be accumulating internally.

- ↘ The number of hours you sleep is the main concern: Sleep quality is another vital element. Fragmented sleep disrupts sleep cycles, cutting off the time spent in the most restorative stages of sleep.

- ↘ Day time sleep compensates for night sleep deprivation: Recent sleep science has proven that you should sleep as much as possible during hours of darkness to align the body's internal clock with the environment.

- ↘ The brain shuts down during sleep: In rapid eye movement (REM) sleep, brain activity reaches peak levels. Sleep is essential for creative thinking, memory, and emotional consolidation.

- ↘ If you can't sleep, stay in bed until it happens: Sleep experts advise getting out of bed if you can't sleep within 20 minutes. In a quiet and dark setting, do a relaxing activity that does not involve lights, screens or any electronic devices. Then try going to bed again.

- ↘ Alcohol before bed improve sleep: The quality of sleep deteriorates significantly with alcohol ingestion. Cutting down on alcohol consumption before bedtime is an imperative sleep hygiene measure.

- ↘ Night exercise delays sleep: Even excessive night exercise does not usually delay sleep. Actually, it helps many people sleep better. But it is preferable to leave a gap of an hour or two between exercise and the planned bedtime to allow the muscles to relax completely.

- ↘ Mattresses last for decades: Like all cushioned furniture, mattresses gradually decline in comfort and support. The Better Sleep Council recommends replacing a mattress every seven years.

References: 112-114.

16

HYPNOGOGIA AND HYPNOPOMPIA

Immersed inside the serenity of a spring evening in Portlligat[50], Salvador Dali sat on his favorite bony Spanish armchair. He stared at the sea and the sweeping horizon beyond, prudently listening to the tranquility of the milieu. After few minutes, he tilted his head back, rested on the stretched leather back of the chair, and hung his hands beyond the chair's arm, positioned in a supine posture of complete relaxation.

In Dali's left hand, he held a heavy key delicately pressed between the extremities of the thumb and forefinger. On the floor, exactly beneath the key, there was a plate turned upside down on the floor.

Slowly, Dali started to doze off, feeling a spiritual drop of anisette of his soul rising in the cube of sugar of his body.

As the stealth of the doze insinuated Salvador's spark of mind for a moment, the key dropped from his fingers, to fall on the upside-down plate, awakening him.

A gush of lurid images, sounds, and sensations conquered the great artist's dizzy mind.

Hurray!!! Hypnogogia is on the run and we have to catch it instantly.

---

50 A small village located in a small bay on the Costa Brava of the Mediterranean Sea, in the municipality of Cadaqués, Catalonia, Spain.

Dali flew off his armchair to the painting easel and started drawing his masterpiece: "The persistence of memory".

Images Dali has seen and felt within his Hypnogogia expressed layers of memories and sensations, which contributed to his genius creativity. The melting clocks in "The Persistence of Memory" are an example of such a product to symbolize the sense of time distortion and drudgery.

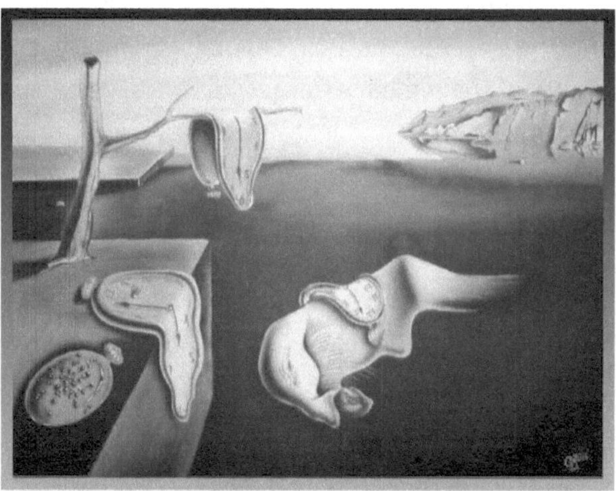

In 2015, Ahmed Elgamma and Babak Saleh from Rutgers University, New Jersey published a "computational framework for assessing the creativity of creative products," ranking thousands of paintings in terms of originality and influence. Dalí came top of the charts.

Hypnogogia is a Greek term that defines the stage of transition from wakefulness to sleep. On EEG, it appears as alpha-theta waves and is characterized by hallucinations, vivid spirit experiences, and lucid dreaming (waking dreams under your control).

Experts who have researched this phenomenon, such as Dorfman, Shames, and Kihlstrom, describe the feelings of the Hypnogogic person to embrace an "absolute knowledge" of enlightenment. The mind creates numerous links between memories, intuitions, emotions, ideas, and triggers from the environment. It produces its own cocktail of "preconscious" state.

Normally, in the transition to sleep, this experience gets lost and forgotten by the time we wake up again. If we can standby at the end of Hypnogogia and then revert to wakefulness, we'll be able to remember and learn from what happened during this stage. It can be accomplished by the right practice and training.

The account above for Dali's "Slumber with a key" technique to catch Hypnogogia was described by the artist himself in his 1948 book *50 Secrets of Magic Craftsmanship*. His concept was to utilize "the taut and invisible wire which separates sleeping from waking" and experience surreal hallucinations not readily available during waking time and easily forgettable when occur amidst deep sleep: "The most characteristic slumber, the one most appropriate to the exercise of the art of painting...is the slumber which I call 'the slumber with a key,' ... you must resolve the problem of 'sleeping without sleeping,' which is the essence of the dialectics of the dream, since it is a repose which walks in equilibrium on the taut and invisible wire which separates sleeping from waking."

Within the book, the famous craftsman underscores empowering of his creativity through sleep:

"You will secretly, in the very depths of your spirit, solve most of your work's subtle and complicated technical problems, which in your state of waking consciousness you would never be humanly capable of solving."

"As you are stretching and yawning voluptuously, you will be able to say to yourself, without fear of falling into exaggeration, that the principal part—that is to say the sleep—of the work is already done."

"An afternoon nap is indispensable to your efficient labors at the end of the day".

These are the keys to the success of Dali's technique:

- It should not be done at the time of real sleep or when you are really tired. Otherwise, you'll be dragged to deep sleep and miss the Hypnogogia.
- It should not be done on a bed or a comfy sofa for the same rationale; escape of Hypnogogia to deep sleep.
- You can use any object that causes noise when it falls on the plate, not necessarily a heavy key.
- The average length of Hypnogogia is five minutes. This is the time window of catching it.
- Try to prepare for it mentally by observing the changing of your consciousness at the start of the nap.
- It needs repetition and habituation according to Salvador's advice: *"To achieve a painter's slumbers will, in fact, require a long period of training"*.

The mirror image of Hypnogogia at the end of sleep is Hypnopompia, the transition from sleep to wakefulness. However, Hypnopompia usually remains much longer than Hypnogogia yet with less intense visions and feelings. The problem with the latter is its occurrence only after a long night sleep. So, it is available only once per 24 hours. Its advantage over Hypnogogia is being easier to catch and practice. The simplest way to hold it can be implemented if we set an alarm 30 minutes earlier than usual in the morning, then we use this half an hour in a practice of balance between sleep and wakefulness. Using the snooze button is quite vital to be sure the next phase is rising up rather than deep sleep.

August Kekule's story of the Benzene molecule mentioned in the previous chapter is another example of Hypnogogia, while Paul

McCartney's story about "Yesterday" is probably an example of Hypnopompia.

Many other artists, writers, scientists, and inventors including Beethoven, Richard Wagner, Walter Scott, Thomas Edison, Nikola Tesla, and Isaac Newton have credited Hypnogogia with boosting their creativity.

David Lynch, a multi-talented genius American filmmaker, painter, guitarist, writer, and actor recommends meditation as an equally brilliant stimulus of creativity. In his book *Catching the Big Fish,* he praises meditation as a pacifier of the exterior sounds and a harmonizer of thoughts. It prepares the mind to a more lively and freer mental flow and opens up for a dimension not normally reached in states occupied by calculated, weighed, and biased thoughts.

Returning the queries and dilemmas raised within the contexts of the previous chapters in relation to dreams:

Are the dream inspirations divine in origin?

Are they just lucky coincidences?

Are they the products or maybe by-products of waking minds consolidated by the sleeping brain?

Can we stimulate change of behavior or induce creativity during time of slumber?

Well, it is rigorously scientific to state that science is still very far away from achieving any solid concrete consensual high-grade evidence in relation to dreams. However, this is a beautiful core of the dilemma. Dreams are by nature out of experimental sight to a great extent. They are the work of the spirit, the soul, and imagination. Although they are still conducted through cells, chemicals, and biology, which can indeed be studied, the end product is too volatile to determine experimentally.

The formation of dreams is a joint work of a person's beliefs, environment, daily life events, fluctuation of feelings, people related, conflicts, joys, worries, hopes, and expectations.

If an artist's mind is pre-occupied with a portrait, a melody, or a movie, these thoughts will be translated in their dreams, which in turn will be transformed to creative work on waking up. The same goes for scientists and inventors. This will remain applicable for people in all professions.

Dreams may exhibit ideas too complex and too exotic to be grasped in a wakeful state.

As shown in this chapter, creative minds not only benefit from their dream experiences by transforming them to a material, but also, they can—to a great extent—stimulate and induce a boost of their creativity.

In terms of behavior change, there have been experiments going on for nearly a century from this perspective. Examples include the nail-biting experiment in the early forties of the 20th century, in which the subjects of the study were dictated during their sleep to stop nail biting with relative success. In another example from the 1950s, California prisoners were dictated during their sleep to stop alcohol intake. The experiment also was concluded with some success. But, in both examples and other recent examples, the change was short-lived.

Reference: 27, 115-118.

Top 10 Dreamland Movies

- 10. Wayne's World 2 (1993): Rated 6.2 on IMDB. The movie plot is kicked off by a dream in which Wayne sees singer Jim Morrison, who tells him to organize a music festival in Aurora, Illinois.

- 9. The Science of Sleep (2006): Rated 7.3 on IMDB. The story of a confused artist troubled by the creativity his vivid dreams provide to him. He loves a French woman and wants to show her his world.

- 8. Eyes Wide Shut (1999): Rated 7.4 on IMDB. A dream state movie in which a New York City doctor boards a harrowing, night-long journey of sexual and moral discovery after his wife reveals that she has been having sexual fantasies with other men.

- 7. Total Recall (1990): Rated 7.5 on IMDB. Douglas Quaid is haunted by a recurring dream about a journey to Mars. He buys a holiday at Rekall Inc. where they sell implanted memories. The implantation becomes faulty and he remembers being a secret agent fighting against the evil Mars administrator.

- 6. A Nightmare on Elm Street (1984): Rated 7.5 on IMDB. Nancy Thompson and a group of her friends are being tortured by a clawed killer in their dreams. Nancy must act quickly, as the killer takes them by turn.

- 5. Open Your Eyes (1997): Rated 7.7 on IMDB. A handsome man finds the love of his life, but he suffers an accident and needs his face rebuilt after it is disfigured. The plot is based on intersecting planes of dream and reality.

- 4. Dreams (1990): Rated 7.8 on IMDB. A collection of stories based upon the actual dreams of director Akira Kurosawa.

- 3. Waking Life (2001): Rated 7.8 on IMDB. A man shuffles through a dream meeting various people and discussing the meanings and purposes of the universe.

2. The Wizard of Oz (1939): Rated 8 on IMDB. A tornado approaches Kansas where Dorothy Gale lives in a farm with her aunt, uncle, and her dog Toto. Dorothy has to seek shelter in her bedroom. The window is blown in and hits her on the head, knocking her unconscious. The house lands in the Land of OZ. After a series of adventures, Dorothy wakes up in her bedroom, surrounded by her family and friends. Everyone dismisses her adventure as a dream, but Dorothy insists it was real.

1. Inception (2010): Rated 8.8 on IMDB. A thief who steals corporate secrets through the use of dream-sharing technology is given the inverse task of planting an idea into the mind of a C.E.O.

Reference: 119.

A CRUISE DOWN THE RIVER GLYMPH

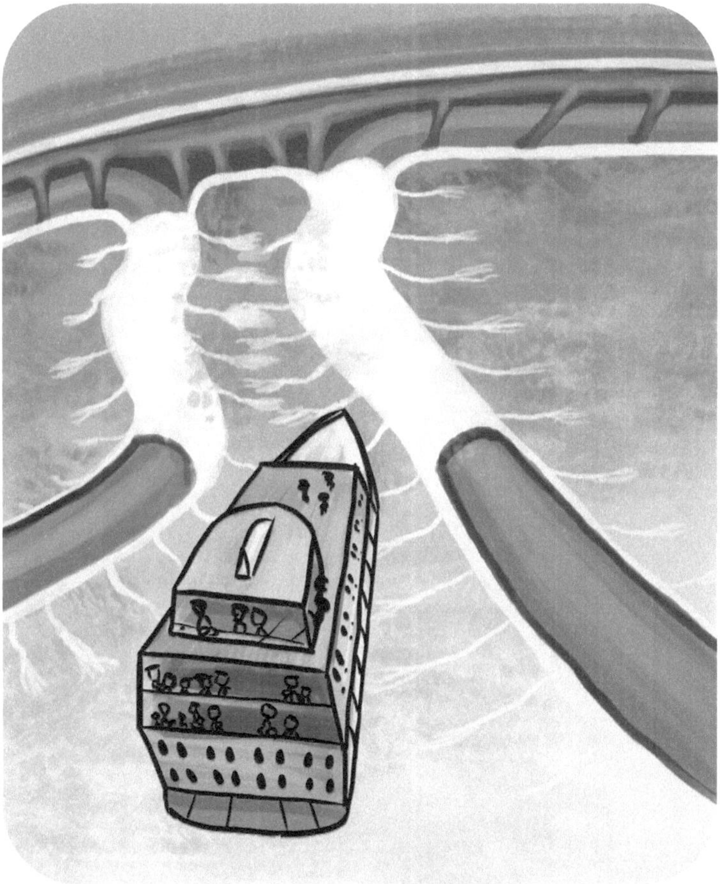

Hello.

Good night, everybody.

My name is Astro and I have the pleasure and honor to be your tour guide for tonight's cruise down the River Glymph.

First, I'd like to thank lady Jamila for hosting us inside her brain on this spectacular occasion.

Lady Jamila has literally just gone to bed as we speak. So, we have to wait at this entry point for few minutes until the gates open.

I'll spend these few minutes talking to you about some History and Geography.

The Glymph River we are cruising tonight is a recent scientific discovery transforming our understanding of how our brains are cleaned as we sleep overnight. This was first introduced to our knowledge a decade or so ago. Doctors and researchers call it the "Glymphatic system."

The water of our river here is the "CSF"[51]. On the banks of the river on both sides, you can see tunnels where the blood flows, blood vessels. Please, beware of this electric network surrounding us. They are all nerves and there are lots of chemicals in between. Touching is forbidden. Otherwise, Lady Jamila's sleep will be disturbed and our cruise will be terminated.

Please join me waving to this chap supervising all the work at the gate. He'll be working hard all night. Let's lift his mood a bit. His name is Melatonin, the sleep hormone. He is considered the maestro of the orchestra here. His work makes you feel drowsy. If you don't, file a complaint to his boss in the pineal body[52].

Ahhhhhh!

Here we are.

I think she is asleep already. The nerves around us are slowing down their charges and becoming very quiescent.

Put on your coats, please. The temperature here will drop in a moment.

Now, as you can see, the river is getting wider and wider. That's because the brain cells are shrinking by about 60% to give us more space. Our gates are open and here we go.

---

51 Cerebrospinal fluid (CSF) is a clear, colorless body fluid found in the brain and spinal cord. There is around 125 mL of CSF at any one time, and about 500 mL is generated every day. CSF acts as a cushion, providing basic mechanical and immunological protection to the brain inside the skull. CSF also serves a vital function in the autoregulation of blood flow inside the brain.

52 The pineal gland is a small gland in the brain of most vertebrates. It produces melatonin, a hormone which regulates sleep patterns. The shape of the gland resembles a pine cone, from which it derived its name. The pineal gland is located near the center of the brain.

If you look at the tunnels on the banks of the river—the blood vessels, as I previously explained—you'll find them now pulsating. This is how these river waves are produced to push our boat and other boats down the river forward.

This lad on the river bank there. Yeah, that big guy. Do you see him? He is a hormone. His name is Cortisol. He'll be going home now and will come back for work in the morning. His job is to open up Lady Jamila's appetite, get her to feel perkier, and to support her to overcome the stress of the day.

As you can see, Cortisol is handing over to his night shift mates. The short guy on the right is called ADH[53]. He'll be going to the lady's kidneys to hold the wee inside until the morning. You don't want to wake up to pee in the middle of the night, do you?

The tall guy on the left is the growth hormone. Oh my GOD! The busiest one of them all. He'll keep on going round and round all the night long; repairing skin and all the muscles and stimulating the hair to get longer. Another hormone will be meeting him near the bones to assist with the recovery of the joints. I hope that lady Jamila's sleep does not get disrupted for the sake of all of her systems.

Ladies and gentlemen, we are now approaching a checkpoint. We'll be passing by lots of these throughout our cruise. Apologies for the disgusting smell. Toxins and waste products from the entire day are now exiting the cells via special channels to the Glymph River through these checkpoints. Can you spot those big brown sacks on

---

53 Anti-diuretic hormone.

the move? They are quite nasty, called amyloids beta. If they stay inside, they cause brain degeneration and Alzheimer's[54].

I can see that cytos have appeared: Hi cytos!

Oh dear! This gang is pretty noisy. Their full name is cytokines. They are on their way to boost her immunity.

Please focus now on the nerves network surrounding you. You'll shortly feel the march of the GABA[55]. Shortly, they'll be on their way to paralyze Lady's Jamila's muscles (apart from her breathing muscles) to restrict her movements so that she can't act out her dreams.

The brain connections are now extremely busy, consolidating the lady's memories.

Oops. The vivid dreams have already started. Please hold tight to the metal bars opposite your seats. From now, no wandering is allowed on the boat. Keep your seatbelts fastened. The tide in the river will now be very high during the stage of rapid eye movement sleep.

The nerve connections are now getting even busier with intensive electric charges and chemical reactions.

Short-term memories are being transformed into long-term memories.

A new map of information is being set in her mind.

---

54 A chronic neurodegenerative disease that gradually worsens over time. It is the cause of 70% of cases of dementia. Initial symptoms are often mistaken for normal ageing. There are to date no medications or supplements that have been proven to reduce the risk.

55 Gamma-Aminobutyric acid is the main inhibitory neurotransmitter in the mammalian central nervous system. Its principal role is reducing neuronal excitability throughout the nervous system.

New connections are established and unnecessary ones are being deleted.

Unwanted emotions are being discarded.

Thank God, it's now settled.

The cycle has ended.

It passed safely.

I hope you enjoyed the cruise.

Those of you who have had enough may get off the boat at the next station.

Those who would like to have another go, you can stay, as the cycle will be repeated all night long. But I am afraid you have to pay for an extra ticket or help with disposal of the nasty amyloids beta.

Your Dreamland Clock

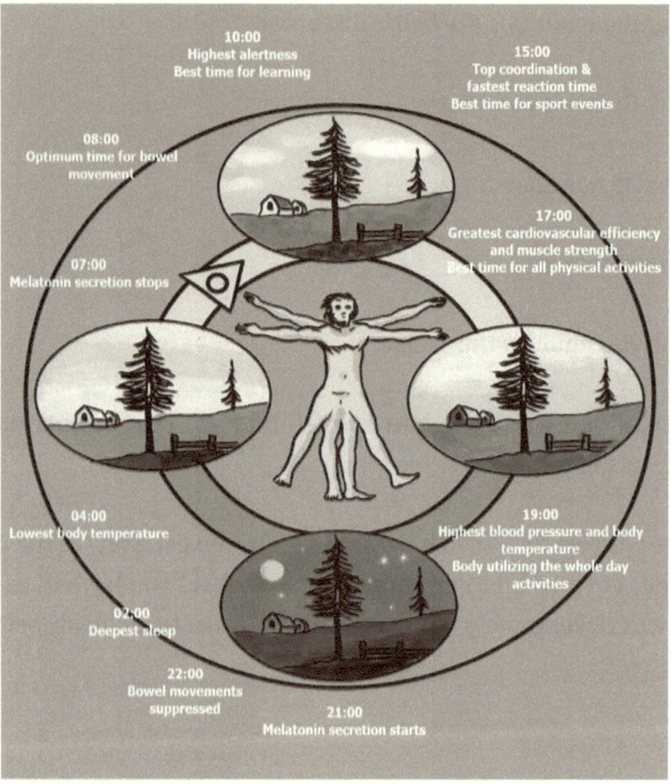

References: 27, 120-127.

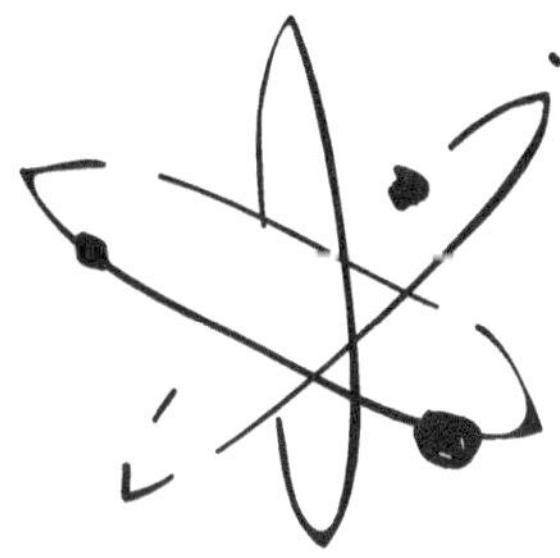

FINALE: THE RESTORATION

Everyone needs a resolution

Some of us are good sleepers, spending a reasonable duration of time in Dreamland enjoying the sweet visions of slumber. The rest often struggle with sleep deprivation and interrupted night rest. Whether you belong to the first group or the latter, a sleep resolution is a rather natural necessity for our contemporary 21st-century lifestyles.

Even if your sleep routine is fine, you will still have nights where you stay up late due to nightmares, unexpected noises, being sick, or having to wake up earlier than usual for a work commitment or even a holiday trip.

Besides, there is always more that we can gain from our kip. Throughout this book, we have explored the stories of people who used their sleep to boost their power, multiply their productivity, and enhance their creativity.

Although we spend one third of our lives asleep (or at least, this what we should do), you scarcely meet anyone determined to make New

Year's resolutions, birthday resolutions, anniversary resolutions, or new life resolutions related to their sleep satisfaction.

But now it is time to invest in the magic of one third of your daily life to achieve the utmost of your potential in the other two thirds.

Your personal tailor

Before trying to implement a resolution for better night sleep, it is imperative to understand that you are your own personal tailor for such an undertaking. Neither this book, nor any other book, website, or a sleep specialist will know your needs, joys, habits, thoughts, pains, commitments, environment, companions, characters, and daily routines better than yourself. The concept is to share the science, the knowledge, the ideas, and the experiences to enlighten the way forward. How, when, and what you use for the practicalities of this endeavor are 100% up to individual personalization.

A 10-dimensions restoration plan

Throughout this book, we have seen how difficult it is to control something so private, so basic, and so vital as your own sleep. The necessity of relaxing in bed every night has been for years an unaffordable luxury for an eminent and rich author like Charles Dickens. Sarvshreshth Gupta[56] committed suicide as he could not manage the time pressure brought by lack of sleep. Michael Jackson's Neverland ranch and a private doctor giving him the most powerful sleep medication could not make his eyes shut down for the night. An Egyptian primary school student[57] missed regularly this basic child's right. Night shift workers all over the world do not have the

---

56 Refer to Chapter 5.

57 Refer to Chapter 10.

luxury of avoiding the health hazards of sleep deprivation. That's why a sleep restoration plan should be multi-dimensional. To succeed in achieving this goal, all dimensions should be considered and complemented.

1. The back-up

In the same way you plan a restoration process for any system, before you start, you need a backup of what you already have. The last thing you want is to lose the valuables you already have. If you have tried something and you know it works for you, please don't lose it. If you are used to a habit endowing a feeling of relaxation at night, keep on practicing it and even enhance it more and more. If a certain smell in your room, a special light effect, or a colorful blanket help you to doze off, do not get rid of them just for the sake of a new start and a reset of your routine. Just integrate them in one way or another in your restoration mode.

2. The set-up

After a heated discussion with your partner, do you expect to be able to sleep within the next 10, 20, 30 minutes?

After you've just shared a post on social media, expecting some likes and comments, do you expect to be able to sleep within the next 10, 20, 30 minutes?

After reading an email from your boss, do you expect to be able to sleep within the next 10, 20, 30 minutes?

The circadian rhythm is not just a clock for chemical reactions. As mentioned in the previous chapter, there is a succession of events orchestrated by melatonin. Our minds, hormones, and vital measurements are in the core of these events; a heated discussion will elevate the body temperature and blood pressure. An exciting post on Facebook will release Adrenaline and wake up the sympathetic system[58]. An email from the boss (whatever its content is) triggers reactions, thoughts, and plans completely opposite to the mindset of a person preparing to rest. A 2018 study conducted by Virginia Tech has shown that just checking work email after hours can cause anxiety and stress[59].

A mindset preparing to rest should do more or less the following:

- Switch all screens off at least one hour before bedtime
- Take a warm bath or shower
- Dim the lights to minimal level
- Do relaxing activities such as reading a book, listening to music, or calm conversation
- Praying/meditation.

In one reliable study, taking a hot bath 90 minutes before bedtime improved sleep quality and helped individuals to have more deep sleep. Even bathing your feet only in warm water makes a difference, according to well-documented research[60]. In another study, a relaxing massage improved sleep quality in ill people[61].

Even just six minutes of reading can reduce stress by 68%, according to research from the University of Sussex[62].

---

58 The division of the nervous system in charge of stimulating the body's fight or flight response. It is described as being antagonistic to the parasympathetic nervous system, which stimulates the body to "feed and breed" and to (then) "rest-and-digest".

59 Reference 128.

60 Reference 129.

61 Reference 130.

62 Reference 131.

In patients of severe insomnia, exercise has proven to be more useful than most sleeping pills, as it reduced time to fall asleep by 55%, total night wakefulness by 30%, and anxiety by 15% while increasing total sleep time by 18%[63]. Yet, exercising too close to bedtime may delay the time to fall asleep, due to increased alertness and activation of the sympathetic system. Thus, the best advice is to exercise early in the evening, finishing at least two to three hours before bedtime.

Keeping the bed for sleep and sex only is a gold standard rule. Lying down there doing work on a laptop or an iPad, watching movies, surfing social media on your phone all interfere with the subconscious correlations of your sleep place. You can choose a sofa in another room for such activities if you prefer to do them in a relaxed position. Besides, it is highly advised not to remain in bed if you can not sleep for more than 20 minutes. If this is the case, get up and spend some time doing a relaxing activity then try again.

There are special relaxation techniques that may help. Detailing them is beyond the spectrum of this book, but you can easily find them by searching the internet.

Suppose that we do all of this and still our minds are occupied at bedtime with all those sorts of stress, anxiety, and concerns.

Are there any other tips for relief?

There are indeed.

One of the tips that may help is to set a time early in the evening to tackle, discuss, and write down notes about everything occupying your mind. Let's call it "Concerns time." Preferably, you should also write down steps you are going to follow the next day or week to

---

63   References 132 & 133.

deal with those concerns. Afterwards, you should engage yourself with other activities until sleep time, so that these concerns do not have space to come back and haunt you in bed.

Writing a "to do" list not related to the concerns shortly before sleep is another excellent tip.

Practicing gratitude has fabulous effects including normalization of blood pressure and reducing risks of depression and anxiety, according to Robert A. Emmons, Professor of Psychology at the University of California, Davis and renowned expert on the science of gratitude. Spending a few minutes close to bedtime in writing down a list of things you are grateful to have is extremely helpful. Mindful prayers can augment the value and benefit of this exercise.

3. The big picture

For most of us, the bigger picture of modern life on this planet is out of our control as individuals. We cannot do much to change our dependance on screens. We cannot do much to change the lifestyles of Lisa Bernard[64], Sarvshreshth Gupta, Samar[65], Mohammed[66], and night shift workers from all professions everywhere in the world.

Such lifestyles are adversely affecting the wellbeing and health of people. Their choices are limited.

If you are reading this book and consider yourself in a position of authority to support students and workers for healthier lifestyles, offering them more choices and flexibility, you would be changing this world for the better. If you can take steps for more social justice

---

64 Refer to Chapter 4.

65 Refer to Chapter 8.

66 Refer to Chapter 10.

in your country, this would be an achievement on its own. As mentioned in Chapter 6 of this book, some companies have been for a decade or so dedicating time and place for naps in the workplace. Changing school times to start later is another recommended change.

If you are reading this book and you do not consider yourself in a position of authority for change, you can at least join support and pressure groups and non-governmental organizations, rallying for more optimum working and learning conditions for all.

4. The clock

You would not arrive late at work due to watching a movie. Would you? If that happened, you would lose your job.

You would not fail to pick up your child from school for the sake of having fun with your friends instead. Would you? If that happened, you would be a negligent parent.

You would not miss your flight to finish playing a football match. Would you? If that happened, your money and holiday would be wasted.

Well, our health and well-being should not be less cherished.

So, sleep is not something we do in our SPARE TIME.

Mr. Melatonin is a figure of authority in your body. He is our night boss, and deserves the same respect we propose to our daytime boss at work.

In insomnia patients, daytime bright light exposure improves sleep quality and duration significantly. In one study, it decreased the time needed to fall asleep by 83%. In another study of older people, it was found that two hours of bright light exposure during the daytime increased the duration of sleep by two hours and enhanced sleep efficiency by 80%[67].

For me personally, I rarely need an alarm to wake up since I have adjusted my sleep and wake up times to be fixed every day, including the weekends.

Sound recommendations by sleep experts to respect the biological clock include the following:

- Trying to go to sleep every night (including the weekends) between 10 PM and 2 AM, and trying to wake up between 6 AM and 8 AM every day.
- Exposure to bright sunlight (to shut down the secretion of melatonin) as soon as you wake up and for at least two hours during the day.
- Reducing your exposure to lights during the night and dimming the lights one hour before going to bed with minimal lights during bedtime (to stimulate the secretion of melatonin).
- No naps after 3 PM.
- Naps before 3 PM should not be longer than 20 minutes each.
- For students, stop homework at least one hour before bedtime.
- Turn off blue lights (radiated by screens) at least one hour before bedtime.

It is difficult to implement all of these changes at once. You'll be able to adopt them successfully if the change is gradual, with maximum timing shift of one to two hours per week.

Of course, all of us may experience occasionally those nights where we cannot adhere to our schedule, either due to urgent work commitments, emergency situations, travel, or even attending a party or

---

67 Reference 134.

a night out. This is not a big deal, as long as it is one night off every now and then and as long as it does not turn into a habit.

There is also some growing evidence supported by a number of sleep specialists that many people may benefit from segmented sleep.

Segmented sleep was the norm before the invention of artificial light (refer to Chapter 2 of this book). In ancient ages, especially in the West, people used to divide their eight hours of sleep into two slots, with two hours of wake up in between for entertainment, meditation, socialization, and sex.

Recent research has proven that it is still healthy to do this, as long as you compile your eight hours by sunrise.

This can be of benefit to workers who return home at 5-7 PM extremely tired. Instead of dozing off half asleep for the evening and then waking up from 2-4 AM until the morning, it would be healthier to have a proper sleep, for example, between 8 PM and 12 AM, then waking up fully between 12 AM and 2 AM, then sleeping fully again from 2 AM until 6 AM.

5. The ambience

The bedtime bedroom environment is vital for the mindset and the sensual harmony of rest. First of all, several studies have pointed out that external noises, usually from traffic, can lead to sleep deterioration and a bunch of health issues.

Image by Arek Socha from Pixabay

In one research study on the bedroom environment of women, around 50% of participants had improved sleep quality when noise and light were diminished[68].

The more impressive scientific findings were related to the room temperature, as it was concluded that this had more effect than noise. A temperature around 20 degrees C (70 F) seems to be the optimum.

Old mattresses are well-known to cause back and shoulder pain. They should be upgraded every six to eight years.

Soft, comfortable sheets and blankets that do not heat overnight also have a substantial role.

A light, nice, calming scent—particularly essential oils with natural aromas, such as lavender—have been known for hundreds of years to ease sleep.

A study presented at the June 2015 SLEEP conference in Seattle suggested that messy bedrooms may contribute to sleep disorders[69].

---

68 Reference 134.

69 Reference 135.

6. Food and drinks

Generally, having a late dinner may negatively affect both sleep quality and the natural release of growth hormone and melatonin.

Some people are more sensitive than others in regard to urination amidst night sleep. For these people, it is better to drink plenty early in the evening and then avoid fluid intake for the last two hours before bed. This way, they will have consumed enough for their requirements and at the same time will avoid sleep disruption for going to the toilet.

Caffeine remains at high levels in the blood for six to eight hours. Therefore, it is not recommended to drink caffeinated beverages in the evening.

Alcohol is known to augment the symptoms of sleep apnea, snoring, and disrupted sleep patterns. It has also a negative effect on melatonin and growth hormone production.

Nicotine similarly has been shown to have a detrimental effect on the quality of slumber.

Refined carbs and sugars are better taken in the first half of the day, as they may induce wakefulness when consumed in the evening. Meanwhile, the best choice of last foods of the day include light, easily digestible crackers and cheese, fruits, or cereals with milk.

7. Medications and natural supplements

Medications and herbal preparations may be one of the solutions for many people with sleep problems. However, there are four scientific facts to be considered before using this kind of help:

i. Although they could be a solution, they are not work of magic on their own. Their role should be only part of the big comprehensive 10-dimension restoration plan. Medications on their own only increase the sleep time by 20-30 minutes.
ii. There are side effects.
iii. They cause dependency; you cannot easily get rid of them in the future if you decide you do not want them anymore.
iv. They are not for everybody. Older people, pregnant and breastfeeding women, people with medical conditions, children, patients taking other medications, etc. should discuss with their doctor to decide if sleep medications are suitable for them, plus which ones to use and for how long.

A July 2018 Consumer Reports survey of 1,767 U.S. adults found out that 80% of the participants had sleep problems at least once a week. About one third of them used a sleep medication[70].

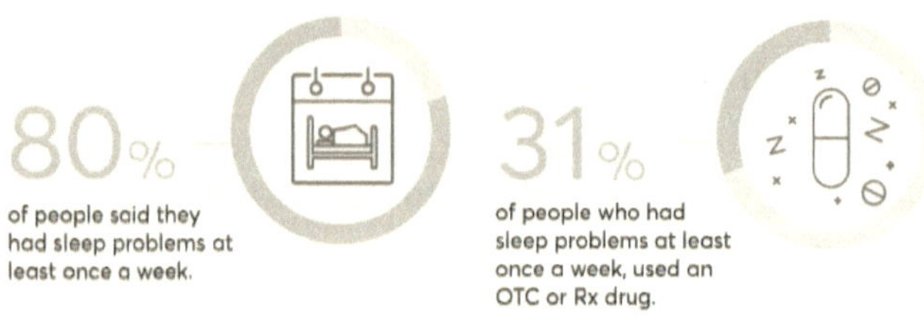

Sleep medications worked for approximately a third of those who used them and made nearly 40% drowsy the next day.

---

70 Reference 136.

Among People Who Used a Sleep Drug

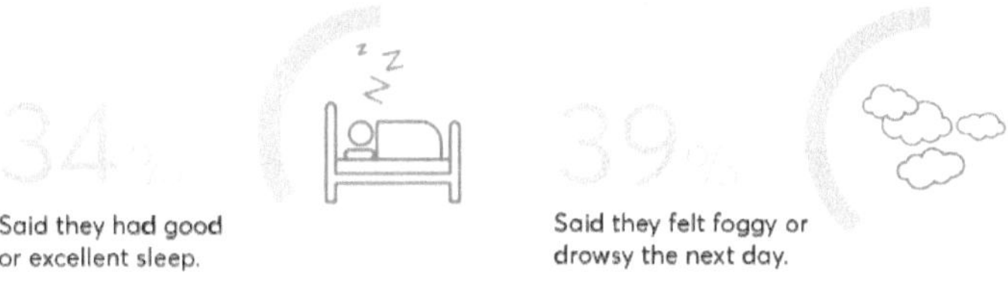

SOURCE: 2018 nationally representative Consumer Reports survey of 1,767 U.S. adults.

Generally, 60% reported side effects, mainly being drowsy or forgetful, confused and unsteady. A few admitted dozing off while driving. A 2015 study published in the American Journal of Public Health looked at the records of nearly 410,000 adults and estimated that drivers taking sleeping pills had a risk of a car crash equivalent to those with an alcohol level over the legal limit.

How do they work?

OTC (over the counter) sleep drugs depend on ingredients like antihistamines—diphenhydramine or doxylamine—which have drowsiness as a side effect.

Prescription medications include anti-anxiety drugs belonging to a class called benzodiazepines or "benzos." They slow the activity of the brain and central nervous system.

The newer generation are called the Z drugs (because they all start with the letter Z). They work on the same receptors, but in a more selective way, reducing the side effects and risk of dependency.

The newest type of prescriptions includes ramelteon and suvorexant, which regulate the sleep-wake cycle, working on brain chemicals.

Another option of treatment is the master himself: Melatonin.

In some studies, taking 2 mg of melatonin 30-60 minutes before bed led to faster sleep with better quality and more energy the next day. Melatonin has no withdrawal effects. The dose can be increased to 5 mg. Its long-term use in children has not been well researched. Nonetheless, melatonin does not work for everybody and loses its positive effect with time. Hence, ideally it should be used only for the short-term, e.g.: when traveling and adjusting to a new time zone for resetting the circadian rhythm.

Logically, if there is an underlying medical condition, the treatment will focus on medications for that condition, e.g., treatment of reflux (regurgitation), depression, obstructive sleep apnea, etc.

If you are more interested in herbal supplements with less dependency and less possibility of side effects (but also less efficacy), 250 mg of Ginkgo biloba one hour before bed has many benefits, aiding relaxation and stress reduction.

500 mg of Valerian root may help you fall asleep and improves sleep quality.

150 mg of lavender can induce a calming and sedentary effect.

In addition to herbs, amino acids like glycine (3 grams) and L-theanine (200 mg) and minerals like magnesium can aid with relaxation, sleep induction, and continuity.

8. Technology

From the invention of artificial light to the development of blue light screens, technology has been always negatively perceived in terms of night sleep. In other words, it was considered to be anti-sleep.

Nonetheless, in the last decade, sleep science has supported many inventions of fabulous worth; a slumber blessing to revert the previous pessimistic perspective.

Here are 10 of the best up-to-date technological inventions to improve sleep quality:

- **Headphones** with apps for white noise, calming natural sounds, or guided relaxation exercises. There are also smart pillows with the same feature if you do not want the headphones.

- **Smart bedroom lights** that dim gradually at night and working the other way around in the morning to mimic the actions of natural sunlight.

- **Eye masks** that beam red lights at the time of sleep and blue lights at the time of wake up (used by astronauts in space where the circadian rhythm and natural lights are lost).

- An **alarm clock** with four integrated sensors to analyze the temperature, sound level, luminosity, and humidity of the room, feeding the accompanying app. Further, there is a sensor for in-depth analysis of sleep duration, cycles, and body movement. A smart watch with the same functions is also available.

- A **duvet** that splits itself in half down the middle, a cooler end and a warmer end for partners who are comfortable with different temperatures.

- An **anti-snoring pillow** that tracks the head position during sleep; when the accompanying speaker detects snoring, airbags in the pillow inflate, adjusting your head until you're breathing normally. The connected app monitors how your sleep has improved.

- A **personalized bed** adjusts the temperature on each side throughout the night, warming and cooling based on the sleeper's natural cycle and preferences. When you get into bed, the feet area warms up to help you fall asleep faster. As your sleep gets deeper, the bed cools down to lower your blood pressure and keep you restful. In the morning, the bed slowly warms up.

- An **app to block blue light** on your laptop, smartphone, or computer.

- A **light therapy box** that radiates bright light, mimicking natural outdoor light. It affects brain chemicals linked to mood and sleep.

- **Weighted blankets** are known for helping to calm children on the autistic spectrum, but they can also help adults manage anxiety and stress. Weighted blankets also promote the production of serotonin which, combats insomnia.

9. Power sleep

Chapter 6 of this book underscored the value of power naps. Power naps restore alertness, boost memory, and promote learning. They enhance both physical and cognitive performance. This becomes particularly relevant with sleep deprivation. The best scientific evidence has proven that power naps enhance efficiency, and lower the risks of heart disease and stroke with improvement of overall health.

To practice power naps in an optimal way, they should be 10-20 minutes only, so that you wake up before entering the deep third stage of slow-wave sleep. Waking up in this stage makes you groggy and disoriented.

During the 10-20 minutes of a power nap, the brain produces sleep spindles, which play a vital role in processing and consolidating memories.

Nap time should be after lunch between 1 and 3PM. Naps after 3PM may disrupt nighttime sleep.

Drinking coffee just before the nap multiplies its benefits.

Ideally, a power nap is taken in a dark quiet place. If this is not possible, eye masks and ear plugs will suffice.

In addition to power naps, the adjustment of daily activities with the circadian rhythm provides the best chance for top performance.

See the illustration at the end of Chapter 17, which shows the most suitable time for each activity; for example, the most apt time for physical activities is between 3 and 5 PM.

10.   Creativity

The same illustration of the finest time for each activity (at the end of Chapter 17) prescribes learning to peak at 10:00 AM, but the rise of cognitive powers actually starts from the last stage of our sleep. This is partially due to the increased release of acetylcholine, a chemical entering the brain, to induce a flexible state in the hippocampus and neocortex[71]. This flexibility allows the neocortex to subconsciously establish connections between seemingly unrelated things.

This blessing of random association may empower people to wake up and solve a problem they've been struggling with, come up with new ideas, finish a project etc. It opens up creativity in addition to thinking outside of the box.

In a 1993 study at Harvard Medical School, psychologist Deidre Barrett asked her students to imagine a problem they were struggling to solve before bedtime. The students successfully came up with rational solutions in their dreams. The published study revealed that 50% of the students reported dreams addressing their chosen problems, while 25% found solutions in their dreams[72].

Image by S. Hermann & F. Richter from Pixabay

Building on what we learnt about the brain activity so far and the most recent robust evidence, night time is not the ideal time for production and creation. However, it can be very useful in reading, gathering information, and discussions. With at least one hour of

---

71 It is a set of layers of the mammalian cerebral cortex involved in higher-order brain functions such as sensory perception, cognition, generation of motor commands, spatial reasoning, and language.

72 Reference 137.

relaxation and winding down after this hard brain work, sleeping on this pool of thoughts gives a brilliant chance for the deep sleep activity to process, connect, and consolidate. When the end of sleep flows into early morning alertness, creativity will peak, producing the brightest solutions and ideas.

Image by Leandro De Carvalho from Pixabay

Psychologist David Watson from the University of Notre Dame monitored 200 participants over three months and found that, at the end of the study, those who scored high on the creativity scale were more able to remember their dreams.

In Chapter 15 and 16 of this book, you read some real stories of geniuses transforming their dreams to achieve splendid milestones for the whole world.

An effective way to remember your dreams is to keep a journal next to your bed during night sleep and next to your armchair during power naps. Gearing up for a hypnopompia or a hypnogogia could be a life-changing opportunity for all of us. Who knows, maybe on day we will enjoy your version of Salvador's Dali "The Persistence of memory" or Paul McCartney's "Yesterday." Perhaps you will be the next Einstein or Mendeleev! If not, at least you can be ecstatic the next morning, proud of your hippocampus' sleep wonders that unraveled your most difficult work imbroglio.

Sleep well!

SOURCES AND REFERENCES

1.   Moore, R.Y., in International Encyclopedia of the Social & Behavioral Sciences, 2001.

2.   Hastings, M.H., Maywood, E.S. & Brancaccio, M. Generation of circadian rhythms in the suprachiasmatic nucleus. Nat Rev Neurosci 19, 453-469 (2018).

3.   Gillette MU & Tischkau SA. Suprachiasmatic nucleus: the brain's circadian clock. Recent Prog Horm Res. 1999; 54:33-58; discussion 58-9. PMID: 10548871.

4.   Huffington, Arianna, The Sleep Revolution: Transforming Your Life, One Night at a Time. Potter/Ten Speed/Harmony/Rodale, 2016.

5.   Craik, Katharine, The 17th Century Guide to Sleep in History Today, 2018.

6.   Hegarty, Stephanie, "The myth of the eight-hour sleep." BBC News, 2012.

7.   Cosnett, J. E., Charles Dickens: Observer of Sleep and Its Disorders, Sleep. 15(3): 264-267, The American Sleep Disorders Association and Sleep Research Society, 1992.

8.   Dickens, Charles, Night Walks, 1860.

9.   Didapper, PJ, How Dickens got a good night's sleep, The Pharmaceutical Journal, 2011.

10. Kryger, Meir, Charles Dickens: Impact on Medicine and Society, Journal of Clinical Sleep: Volume 8, Issue 3, Medicine, 2012.

11. The Active Times, Bizarre Sleeping Habits of Famous People, 2018.

12. Martin, Emmie, 14 bizarre sleeping habits of super-successful people, The Independent, 2016.

13. Rasicot, Jolie, We don't know how she does it, Bethesda Magazine: March-April 2014.

14. Calhoun, Ada, Gen X Women Get Less Sleep Than Any Other Generation. What's Keeping Them Up? Time, 2020.

15. Fleming, John, Gallup Analysis: Millennials, Marriage and Family, 2016.

16. Livingston, Gretchen & Cohn, D'vera, Childlessness Up Among All Women; Down Among Women with Advanced Degrees, PEW Research Center, 2010.

17. Women and Anxiety, Anxiety and Depression Association of America website.

18. Broster, Alice, Anxiety Disorder: Women Are Twice As Likely To Be Diagnosed And Should Be Screened To Improve Detection, Treatment, Suggests Health Coalition, Forbes, 2020.

19. Worley, Will, Women need more sleep than men because of their 'complex' brains, research suggests, The Independent, 2016.

20. Pien, Grace Weiwei, How Does Menopause Affect My Sleep? Johns Hopkins Medicine website.

21. Szkiela, Marta et al. "Night Shift Work-A Risk Factor for Breast Cancer." International journal of environmental research and public health, vol. 17, 2, 659. 20 Jan. 2020.

22. Schernhammer, Eva S., et al., Rotating Night Shifts and Risk of Breast Cancer in Women Participating in the Nurses' Health Study, JNCI: Journal of the National Cancer Institute, Volume 93, Issue 20, October 17, 2001, Pages 1563–1568.

23. Chakraborty, Angshukanta, Goldman Sachs analyst death: How the rush burns out our brightest, in Daily O, 2015.

24. Eshwar, Bart, Overwork Led To The Death Of Sarvshreshth Gupta, Office Chai, 2015.

25. Sorkin, Andrew Ross, Reflections on Stress and Long Hours on Wall Street, The New York Times, 2015.

26. ENS Economic Bureau, 22-year-old Indian analyst's death in US sparks debate on long working hours, The Indian Express, 2015.

27. Wikipedia pages related to the subject.

28. Pepitone, Julianne, Co-founder of social network Diaspora dies at 22, CNN, 2011.

29. Muncy, Jeremy, Ilya Zhitomirskiy Update: Reports Show Diaspora Co-Founder Committed Suicide, Web Archive, 2011.

30. Kennedy, Maev, Moritz Erhardt death: Intern's parents feared he was exhausted at work, The Guardian, 2013.

31. Miller, Stephen & Dolmetsch, Chris, Thomas Hughes, Moelis & Co. Banker, Dies at 29 in Building Fall, Bloomberg, 2015.

32. Tiwari, Sandali, Britannica COO suicide: Friends, kin recall inspirational Vineet Whig, The Indian Express, 2016.

33. CBS news, Kate Spade died from suicide by hanging, medical examiner says, 2018.

34. Carras, Christi, Kate Spade's Husband Issues Statement: She 'Suffered From Depression and Anxiety', Variety, 2018.

35. Kerr, Breena, Depression Among Entrepreneurs is an Epidemic Nobody is Talking About, The Hustle, 2015.

36. Newsom, Rob, Depression and sleep, Sleep Foundation website, updated 2020.

37. Levine, David, Why Sleep Deprivation Eases Depression? Scientific American, 2013.

38. Geddes, Linda, Staying awake: The surprisingly effective way to treat depression, Mosaic Science, 2018.

39. Davis, Jeanie Lerche, Dreams May Hold Key to Beating Depression, WebMD, 2002.

40. Rush University Medical Center, Dreams may provide glimpse into subconscious of divorced depressed patients, 2002.

41. Weinstein, Henry, A Sleeping Lawyer and a Ticket to Death Row, Los Angeles Times, 2000.

42. Blakinge, Keri, Judge rejects appeal from Houston death row prisoner whose lawyer slept during trial, Houston Chronicle, 2019.

43. Weiss, Debra Cassens, Sleeping lead lawyer doesn't justify overturning capital conviction, federal judge rules, ABA Journal, 2019.

44. Grasshopper resources, Power Naps: The Secret Weapon Your Business Might Be Missing.

45. BBC NEWS, Should workers be allowed to nap at work? 2019.

46. Kroll-Smith, Steve, Modern Work and the Sleepy Worker, Virtual Mentor. 2008; 10(9): 589-593. doi: 10.1001/virtualmentor.2008.10.9.msoc2-0809.

47. Whitfield, John, Naps for Better Recall, Scientific American, 2008.

48. Short, Michelle A & Banks, Siobhan, Sleep Deprivation and Disease (pp.13-26), The Functional Impact of Sleep Deprivation, Sleep Restriction, and Sleep Fragmentation, 2014.

49. Derickson, Alan, Dangerously Sleepy: Overworked Americans and the Cult of Manly Wakefulness, University of Pennsylvania Press, 2014.

50. Greusel, John Hubert, Thomas A. Edison: The Man, His Work and His Mind, 1913.

51. Coren, Stanley, Sleep Thieves, 1997.

52. Dyer, Frank Lewis, Thomas Edison: His Life and Inventions, CreateSpace Independent Publishing Platform, 2015.

53. Harvard T.H. Chan school of public health, Sleep and obesity.

54. Bonanno, Lilla MSc, PhDa et al., Assessment of sleep and obesity in adults and children, Medicine: November 2019, Volume 98, Issue 46, p. e17642.

55. University of Warwick. "Sleep deprivation: Late nights can lead to higher risk of strokes and heart attacks, study finds." ScienceDaily. ScienceDaily, February 8, 2011.

56. Watson, Stephanie & Cherne, Kristeen, The Effects of Sleep Deprivation on Your Body, Healthline, 2020.

57. Peri, Camille, 10 Things to Hate About Sleep Loss, WebMd Archives.

58. Finan, Patrick, The Effects of Sleep Deprivation, Johns Hopkins Medicine website.

59. Albayan UAE newspaper.

60. Alwatan Egyptian newspaper.

61. The World Bank, Nearly Half the World Lives on Less than $5.50 a Day, press release October 2018.

62. OXFAM, The 22 richest men in the world have more wealth than all the women in Africa, 2020.

63. OXFAM, Not all gaps are created equal: The true value of care work.

64. Viter Energy, For doctors and nurses, long hours mean more errors, 2016.

65. Wible, Pamela, The secret horrors of sleep-deprived doctors, Kevin MD, 2017.

66. CC., Caruso, Negative impacts of shiftwork and long work hours. Rehabil Nurs. 2014; 39(1): 16-25.

67. Stimpfel AW, Sloane DM, Aiken LH. The longer the shifts for hospital nurses, the higher the levels of burnout and patient dissatisfaction. Health Aff (Millwood). 2012; 31(11): 2501-2509.

68. Lockley SW et al., Harvard Work Hours, Health and Safety Group. Effects of health care provider work hours and sleep deprivation on safety and performance. Jt Comm J Qual Patient Saf. Nov 2007; 33(11 Suppl): 7-18.

69. Khazan, Olga, When You Can't Afford Sleep, The Atlantic, 2014.

70. Home CEU, Lack of Sleep Symptoms in Healthcare Workers Leads to Safety Dangers.

71. Brumfield, Ben, Shift workers beware: Sleep loss may cause brain damage, new research says, CNN health, 2014.

72. Kelley, Paul et al., Is 8:30 a.m. Still Too Early to Start School? A 10:00 a.m. School Start Time Improves Health and Performance

of Students Aged 13–16, Front. Hum. Neurosci., December 8, 2017.

73. Urton, James, Teens get more sleep, show improved grades and attendance with later school start time, researchers find, UW news, 2018.

74. Lee, Katherine, More Evidence Finds That Delaying School Start Times Improves Students' Performance, Attendance, and Sleep, Everyday Health, 2018.

75. Newport Academy website, The Latest on Teen Cell Phone Addiction, 2017.

76. Henry Ford Health System Staff, Can 30 More Minutes Of Sleep A Day Make A Difference? Henry Ford live well, 2017.

77. Wheaton, Anne G et al. "School Start Times, Sleep, Behavioral, Health, and Academic Outcomes: A Review of the Literature." The Journal of school health vol. 86, 5 (2016): 363-81.

78. Fiorenzi, Ryan, Sleep Needs by Age and Gender, Start Sleeping website, 2020.

79. Clun, Rachel, Experts reveal new sleep requirements for different age groups, The Sydney Morning Herald, 2015.

80. National Sleep Foundation Recommends New Sleep Times, 2015.

81. Duke, Alan, Nurse details Michael Jackson's fatal search for sleep, CNN, 2013.

82. Associated Press, AEG Live Not Responsible in Death of Michael Jackson, Billboard, 2013.

83. Associated Press, Concert promoter found NOT GUILTY of negligence by hiring Conrad Murray to treat Michael Jackson, Daily Mail, 2013.

84. Duke, Alan, Lawsuit evidence: Michael Jackson lost dance moves in last days, CNN, 2013.

85. ABC7, Michael Jackson wrongful death trial: Potentially damaging emails surface, 2013.

86. Duke, Alan, Expert: Michael Jackson went 60 days without real sleep, CNN, 2013.

87. Suni, Eric, Stages of sleep, Sleep Foundation, 2020.

88. Higuera, Valencia, What Is Kleine-Levin Syndrome (KLS)? Healthline, 2018.

89. Lanese, Nicoletta, Girl with Rare 'Sleeping Beauty' Syndrome Dozes for Months, Live Science, 2019.

90. Hall, Joe, With the help of seizure medication, Wyatt Shaw is once again the life of the party, Norton Children's, 2018.

91. Alvarez, Jason, After 10-Year Search, Scientists Find Second 'Short Sleep' Gene, University of California San Francisco, 2019.

92. Campbell, A Third "Short Sleep" Gene Has Been Discovered – And It Prevents Memory Deficits, Technology Networks, 2019.

93. Parth Shah et al, Eleven Days Without Sleep: The Haunting Effects Of A Record-Breaking Stunt, WBUR, 2019.

94. City News, Man Acquitted Of Sleepwalking Murder Running For School Trustee In Durham, 2006.

95. Brogaard, Berit, Sleep Driving and Sleep Killing, Psychology Today, 2012.

96. Providentia, The Sleepwalker Defense, 2020.

97. Supreme Court of Canada judgements, R.V. Parks, 1992.

98. Shearer, Lloyd, He killed in his sleep, Ottawa Citizen, 1961.

99. Martin, Lawrence, Can sleepwalking be a murder defense? Lakeside Press, 2009.

100. BBC News, Sleepwalker' accused of murder, March 2005.

101. Steven Morris, Devoted husband who strangled wife in his sleep walks free from court, The Guardian, 2009.

102. Hadwin, Lee. https://www.leehadwin.com/

103. Dafoe, Taylor, Lee Hadwin Never Dreamed of Being an Artist. To His Surprise, He Becomes One in His Sleep, Artnet News, 2019.

104. BBC, The mysterious case of the man who draws in his sleep.

105. Zaidel DW. Creativity, brain, and art: biological and neurological considerations. Front Hum Neurosci. 2014; 8: 389. Published Jun 2, 2014.

106. Ingravallo F, Poli F, Gilmore EV, et al. Sleep-related violence and sexual behavior in sleep: a systematic review of medical-legal case reports. J Clin Sleep Med. 2014; 10(8): 927-935. Published Aug 15, 2014.

107. Fleetham JA, Fleming JA. Parasomnias. CMAJ. 2014; 186(8): E273-E280.

108. Singh S, Kaur H, Singh S, Khawaja I. Parasomnias: A Comprehensive Review. Cureus. 2018;10(12):e3807. Published Dec 31, 2018.

109. Mahowald, Mark W.; Schenck, Carlos H., Insights from studying human sleep disorders, Nature, Volume 437, Issue 7063, pp. 1279-1285 (2005).

110. Confusional Arousals—Overview and Facts, Sleep Education website.

111. Sat Sharma, Disorders That Disrupt Sleep (Parasomnias), E-Medicine Health, reviewed 2019.

112. Parker, Steve, Einstein's dream, Jung Currents.

113. The Spaced Out-Scientist, Dreams and visions in scientific innovation, 2015.

114. Turner, Rebecca, 10 Dreams That Changed Human History, World Of Lucid Dreaming.

115. Carr, Michelle, How to Dream Like Salvador Dali? Psychology Today, 2015.

116. Charles, David, 'Sleeping Without Sleeping': How To Create Like Salvador Dalí, Medium, 2010.

117. Baer, Drake, Salvador Dali mastered the power nap and you should too, Business Insider, 2016.

118. Yetman, Daniel, What Is Hypnagogia, the State Between Wakefulness and Sleep? Healthline, 2020.

119. IMDB website.

120. Bacyinski A, Xu M, Wang W, Hu J. The Paravascular Pathway for Brain Waste Clearance: Current Understanding, Significance and Controversy. Front Neuroanat. 2017; 11: 101. Published Nov 7, 2017.

121. Louveau A, Smirnov I, Keyes TJ, et al. Structural and functional features of central nervous system lymphatic vessels [published correction appears in Nature. May12, 2016; 533(7602): 278]. Nature. 2015; 523(7560): 337-341.

122. Jessen NA, Munk AS, Lundgaard I, Nedergaard M. The Glymphatic System: A Beginner's Guide. Neurochem Res. 2015; 40(12): 2583-2599.

123. Aspelund A, Antila S, Proulx ST, et al. A dural lymphatic vascular system that drains brain interstitial fluid and macromolecules. J Exp Med. 2015; 212(7): 991-999.

124. Iliff JJ, Wang M, Liao Y, et al. A paravascular pathway facilitates CSF flow through the brain parenchyma and the clearance of interstitial solutes, including amyloid β. Sci Transl Med. 2012; 4(147): 147ra111.

125. Xie L, Kang H, Xu Q, et al. Sleep drives metabolite clearance from the adult brain. Science. 2013; 342(6156): 373-377.

126. Ng Kee Kwong KC, Mehta AR, Nedergaard M, Chandran S. Defining novel functions for cerebrospinal fluid in ALS pathophysiology. Acta Neuropathol Commun. 2020; 8(1): 140. Published Aug 20, 2020.

127. Abbott, N.J., Pizzo, M.E., Preston, J.E. et al. The role of brain barriers in fluid movement in the CNS: is there a 'glymphatic system?. Acta Neuropathol 135, 387–407 (2018).

128. Virginia Tech, Mere expectation of checking work email after hours harms health of workers and families, Science Daily, 2018.

129. UT News, Take a Warm Bath 1-2 hours Before Bedtime to Get Better Sleep, Researchers Find, University of Texas website, 2019.

130. Richards KC. Effect of a back massage and relaxation intervention on sleep in critically ill patients. Am J Crit Care. Jul 1998; 7(4): 288-99.

131. Jessica Mansourati, Want To Reduce Your Stress Levels By 68% In 6 Minutes? Read A Book, Medium 2019.

132. Passos GS, Poyares DL, Santana MG, Tufik S, Mello MT. Is exercise an alternative treatment for chronic insomnia? Clinics (Sao Paulo). 2012; 67(6): 653-660.

133. Passos GS, Poyares D, Santana MG, Garbuio SA, Tufik S, Mello MT. Effect of acute physical exercise on patients with chronic primary insomnia. J Clin Sleep Med. Jun 15, 2010; 6(3): 270-5.

134. Rudy Mawer, 17 Proven Tips to Sleep Better at Night, Healthline 2020.

135. Davies, Madlen, How a MESSY ROOM affects your sleep: Hoarders take longer to nod off and are more dozy in the daytime, Mail Online, 2015.

136. Carr, Teresa, The Problem With Sleeping Pills, Consumer Reports, 2018.

137. Barrett, Deirdre, The "Committee of Sleep": A Study of Dream Incubation for Problem Solving, Dreaming, Vol. 3, No. 2, 1993.

138. Kluger, Jeffrey, How to Wake Up To Your Creativity, Time, 2017.